## THE EVENING OF THE HOLIDAY

Shirley Hazzard was born and educated in Sydney, Australia. She has lived in the Far East, New Zealand, and Italy, and now lives in New York with her husband, the writer Francis Steegmuller. She worked at the United Nations for ten years, resigning in 1962 to become a full-time writer. She has written five other books: four works of fiction and *Defeat of an Ideal*, a study of the United Nations. Many of her short stories have been published in *The New Yorker*, and she has received a First Prize in the O. Henry Short Story Awards. Her novel *The Transit of Venus* won the National Book Critics Circle Award for the best novel of 1980.

Shirley Hazzard

# The Evening of
# the Holiday

A KING PENGUIN
PUBLISHED BY PENGUIN BOOKS

PENGUIN BOOKS
Published by the Penguin Group
Viking Penguin Inc., 40 West 23rd Street,
New York, New York 10010, U.S.A.
Penguin Books Ltd, 27 Wrights Lane,
London W8 5TZ, England
Penguin Books Australia Ltd, Ringwood,
Victoria, Australia
Penguin Books Canada Ltd, 2801 John Street,
Markham, Ontario, Canada L3R 1B4
Penguin Books (N.Z.) Ltd, 182–190 Wairau Road,
Auckland 10, New Zealand

Penguin Books Ltd, Registered Offices:
Harmondsworth, Middlesex, England

First published in the United States of America by
St. Martin's Press 1966
First published in Great Britain by Macmillan Ltd 1966
Published in Penguin Books 1988

LIBRARY OF CONGRESS CATALOGING IN PUBLICATION DATA
Hazzard, Shirley, 1931–
The evening of the holiday.
Reprint. Originally published: London: Macmillan;
New York: St. Martin's Press, 1966.
I. Title.
PR9619.3.H369E94    1988    823    87-32823
ISBN 0 14 01.0451 8

Printed in the United States of America by
R. R. Donnelley & Sons Company, Harrisonburg, Virginia
Set in Linotype Pilgrim

*For Francis*

Questo dì fu solenne: or da' trastulli prendi
riposo.
GIACOMO LEOPARDI
*La Sera del Dì di Festa*

# One

'Tancredi,' Gabriella said to her brother, 'you must show them the fountain.'

'All in good time, my dear,' he replied irritably. 'Let's have our tea in peace.'

They were not really having tea; the word referred only to the hour. Italians are not good at entertaining in their houses in the late afternoon. It is precisely the time when they would normally be rousing themselves from the siesta and looking forward to the evening in the café. Also, they don't quite know what to serve; tea, if done properly, should be an ambitious affair with cakes and scones, which they would not dream of providing, and they have never pretended to be sherry drinkers, which would be the convenient way out. So one is likely to be confronted, as on this afternoon, with half a bottle of sweet vermouth and a plateful of stale macaroons.

Tancredi had grown up in Sicily, where no entertaining is ever done in the summer afternoons, where there is a solitary, almost therapeutic drinking of lemonade or almond milk in darkened rooms before the sun goes down. He regarded the afternoon as something to be slept through. Here in the north, however, shops and businesses reopened early, at four o'clock. He was an architect and his work was not much affected by the summer exodus;

on any other day he would have evaded the tea party by returning to his office in the town. But today there was a religious holiday, the feast of the Ascension, and here he was pinned to a sofa among the women and the aged, like someone left behind during a war.

He had been staying here in his sister's house since the early spring. The reason he gave for this arrangement, to others and sometimes to himself, was the proximity of the house to the town – his own villa was well out in the countryside – and the company it gave his sister. However, as he had travelled back and forth to his villa for years without mentioning the inconvenience, and as his attitude towards his sister left something to be desired in the way of companionship, it was generally assumed that he found his deserted house intolerable since his wife had left him. In the town it was felt to be a great pity that such a beautiful house should stand empty – but for years the *architetto* and his wife had been ... (here a gesture of two hands going in completely opposite directions). Now she had actually left him and gone to her family's house at the sea (another gesture, signifying money on all sides), and taken the children. Ah, the poor *architetto* (and now a sign to the effect that money wasn't everything), he missed his children, and *that* was why he had moved in with his sister.

The mention of tea brought the contents of the tray to Tancredi's attention. He looked down with distaste and saw that the maid had laid the tray, unsuitably, with heavy linen napkins and, uselessly, with slightly tarnished cake forks. 'Look at the way she's set the tray,' he grumbled in front of the visitors. 'Anyone would think we were a lot of bourgeois Neapolitans.'

His sister, who was rather afraid of him, was unable to

pass this off as another woman might have done with a little good-natured clucking. She looked anxiously at the tray, then apologetically back at him. Her delicate expression of long-suffering lengthened. The guests – an old painter and his wife, and the young woman they had brought with them – stared discreetly into the air above the tea table.

'Our wine,' Tancredi burst out. 'You'd prefer our wine.' The wine, which was from his own land, was one of the best in the district.

But no, no – at once they began to protest, if not in so many words, that vermouth and stale macaroons more than met their needs. Only the foreign woman fully understood and asked him for a glass of wine, and he got up to fetch it. He brought it back and took his place again beside her on the sofa. (His sister had in fact asked him to sit next to the old man, the painter Giovanetti, whom he had known all his life but now rarely saw, but he had managed to change places by getting up to help when the tray was brought in – an intervention that earned him a look of mild surprise from the maid.) Now Gabriella was chatting with the old couple. They were visiting the town for two or three days from their home at Lucca.

Old Giovanetti, sitting upright in a plush armchair, clasped both hands over the knob of a black walking stick that was planted between his feet. In this attitude he was like an old crusader, his noble face and his long, lean body and his stillness conveying some figure on a perpendicular tomb. He was almost eighty – many years older than Renata, his wife – and he put at a disadvantage the rest of the company, who could never hope to survive so well. Renata and Gabriella were both a little voluble, a little

9

heavy, a little too handsomely dressed – in silk dresses with matching jackets – for the warm spring afternoon. They were well educated, pious women, and much of their conversation was taken up with illustrating the fundamental worth of human nature – a quality not always susceptible of illustration and, when illustrated, not always interesting. For all their chatter, they exuded less vitality than the old man sitting silent between them.

Tancredi himself, in his forties, already had rather more flesh and slightly less hair than the old man and, although conventionally handsome, he lacked any particular physical distinction. This afternoon, for the first time, he had become aware of that discrepancy; it was one reason he had changed places.

And the woman on the sofa, to whom he now handed a too full glass of wine – Tancredi shrugged in his mind: she was nothing extraordinary either. It seemed that she had known the Giovanettis years ago in Lucca, and Tancredi had met her yesterday when he called at their hotel in the town. She herself was spending some weeks here, she said, staying at the hotel. She had relatives in this area whom she visited from time to time – and he had been surprised, when he asked the name of these relatives, to discover that he knew her aunt, a Signora Brandi, a woman now grown old, a widow, well known to him and famous in that countryside for her beauty and character. He was afraid he had looked rather *too* surprised – there was so little resemblance. Then, too, the discovery that she was half Italian had come just as he was deciding that she was the archetypal Englishwoman. No, she was nothing special; only she had those startling green eyes that were rare in this country. Otherwise, a fair head, a thin neck, and attenuated arms that today were covered almost to the wrist by the cuffed sleeves of the dress she wore. The dress, patterned with narrow mauve and white stripes, had a high collar too, but yesterday he had noticed the shape of her shoulders and the prominent bones below her throat. As she set her glass on the table, a fine gold bracelet slipped out of her sleeve and along her wrist.

'What is the fountain?' she suddenly asked Tancredi.

He said: 'It's down in the garden, behind the house. Oh – an old thing, you know, marble, rather decrepit. But it's nicely placed, and has been attributed to a design of Pisano. Not that that means anything,' he added hastily. 'It's only conjecture, and would hardly affect the thing's appearance if it were proved.' He took out his handkerchief and dried the table, which was splashed with the overflow of wine. 'Certainly it wasn't executed by Pisano. It may be even older.'

'Perhaps we can see it later,' she said.

She was called Sophie. He had not understood her Christian name when they first said it to him, but as they were all going out of the hotel together yesterday there was a message for her at the desk, and he had seen her name written on the outer fold of the paper. 'Signorina,' he began now, so that she would not find the rest of the remark too familiar, 'you have a Greek name.'

'How nice to think of it that way,' she said, smiling at him.

'Have you been in Greece?'

'Never. When I get away I come to Italy.'

'How did you know the Giovanettis?'

'I was at college in Florence,' she explained, 'with their daughter Sibilla.'

'Ah yes, Sibilla,' he said.

'She married a Dutchman at the United Nations – I suppose you know. They went to live in Africa.'

'Yes,' he said. 'In Mogadiscio.' It happened that he had at one time been rather in love with this same Sibilla and was both pleased and sorry to be reminded of her now. They had carried on a long flirtation, quite unsuspected by his wife; after Sibilla's marriage they kept vaguely in touch. And when she went to Mogadiscio he sent her letters, to which she never replied; he wondered if she had even received them. (These letters had, in fact, reached Sibilla and greatly amused her, bored as she was on that splendid, lonely coast of East Africa. She had written a long and indiscreet reply, which the Somali houseboy had thrown away instead of posting, having first removed the stamps for resale.) The thought of Sibilla – who was more beautiful than this girl – and of his unanswered letters now began to depress Tancredi. In his heart he sighed. What an afternoon.

'What were you studying in Florence?' he asked, making an effort. As though, he said to himself, they ever study anything but History of Art.

'Oh –' She laughed. 'I had real pretensions. I wrote a paper on Anita Garibaldi.'

At this moment Gabriella asked him to refill their glasses, and he got up again and went around the low table with the bottle in his hand. When he came back this Sophie was ready to talk of something else, but he sat down and said after a pause: 'Anita Garibaldi then. I have a little association with Anita Garibaldi.'

Now he was leaning forward, his right elbow on his knee, and she leaned back to put more distance between them.

'There's a monument in Rome,' he went on, 'to Anita Garibaldi.'

'On the Janiculum.'

'You know it, of course. Well, in 1932 or -3, it must have been – at any rate while I was at the University – they were raising money in Rome to erect that monument. I was a penniless student and I knew almost nothing about Anita Garibaldi. But it was at a time when there was precious little one could subscribe to, in any case, and I subscribed to that.'

'How nice,' she said, lifting her head. I was one year old, she thought.

'I suppose it appealed to my romantic notions,' he said, and smiled. 'Though I would hate to tell you how little I gave. And it would sound even worse to you,' he added, 'when one considers what has happened to the lira since then.' However, she was delighted. The distant gesture on behalf of the monument, which he had as good as forgotten, now quite seemed to him to have been ordained for this moment. The sagging room righted itself before his eyes. He felt that, if he particularly wanted to, he could make a conquest of this Sophie. The word 'conquest' had reality to him – he liked the idea of supremacy and believed, correctly, that women want to be prevailed upon; since he was not puritanical, this conquest did not necessarily imply to him one single carnal objective. 'Garibaldi's wife, however, is an unusual instance,' he continued. 'In Italy women are not encouraged to be so enterprising. In England, of course, there have been so many heroic women.' He groped for a name or two. 'Boadicea, and . . .' Eighteen centuries slipped through his grasp. 'Florence Nightingale. We Latins are rather to be criticized on that account – we tend to keep women inside the house.' And an excellent thing too, he added to himself.

'It's probably a very good thing,' she said.

But even this remark struck him as a bit too opinionated for his taste. He hoped she wasn't going to be full of theories. Even the term 'a clever woman' was disagreeable to him; one said 'a clever man' in commendation, but 'a clever woman' had a pejorative sound to it. 'Oh, surely not,' he said perversely. 'Women should want to be independent.'

But she laughed and turned away, taking up her glass. 'I thought you said you were a romantic.'

'Oh,' he cried, pleased with her again. 'Is this to be one of those days when everything you say is remembered and used against you?'

'One of those days?' She looked back at him over the glass, still smiling. 'I shouldn't have thought there was any other kind of day.'

'In any case, I intended that against myself, you know. I meant to say that I was sentimental.'

'It didn't sound as if you thought it such a fault,' she said.

'Ah no, you're right. We only accuse ourselves of what we really find rather attractive – or at least bearable. We say: "I'm too easy-going," or too soft-hearted, or too honest, or too ingenuous.' He made a dismissing gesture with his right hand, and then extended it towards her. 'Isn't that so, signorina? Isn't it so?'

'Tancredi,' Gabriella called from the other side of the table. He felt, as it were, apprehended – leaning towards this Sophie, appealing to her with his open hand. 'Tancredi, Renata says they have to go soon. Do take them into the garden first. Do walk down to the fountain with them.'

'Is it far?' the old painter interrupted, looking at his wife. 'I don't remember.'

Tancredi swung round on the sofa, almost turning his back on the Sophie woman, publicly repudiating her soft, concentrating look, which was still arranged for his benefit, he felt. 'Not far. Not far at all. Down the steps – don't you remember? On the other side of the arbour. It'll do you good. Why,' he went on with an over-hearty diplomacy, 'if you begin to make excuses, I'll think you want to stay here alone with Gabriella.'

They all smiled indulgently, as if the old man were a child. He looked at them aloofly. His wife, bending towards him, said archly: 'Are you going to let that pass?'

He shrugged, as if he hadn't understood. 'Let it pass? Let what pass? All my life people have been trying to whip me into indignation. Women are especially bad that way. "You aren't going to let this pass," "You can't let that pass" – when all I *want* is to let it pass.' He leaned forward in his seat, his hands clasping the silver knob of his stick. 'To let everything pass.'

There was an uneasy silence. 'If it's really too far for him –' Tancredi began, and paused.

'Not a bit of it,' said Renata cheerfully. 'He's the youngest of all of us.'

'When people say that,' the old man told her, 'I know I must really be on my last legs.' He got up without any suggestion of effort and stood leaning on his stick while the others gathered themselves together.

Renata took Gabriella by the arm. 'Aren't you coming?'

'I? Oh, I don't do those steps more often than I can help,' she said. 'Not with my arthritis.'

How long women take to leave a room, Tancredi thought. They can't simply get up and walk out – all this shambling and turning back on their tracks, chattering and embracing, talking of their arthritis. His heart sank again. We are all thickened with middle age, he thought. We have let everything pass.

They came at last through double doors on to a sunlit terrace, a flagged square at the top of the steep flight of steps. There was more talk with Gabriella, who now would not come out in the sun. The old man looked at the steps and shook his head. 'I don't remember any of this,' he said.

'Nothing is new,' Tancredi said – not humorously, although the stairs and the urns decorating the stone railing were flaked and dinted with great age and the flagstones yellowed with a fine sheen of moss. 'You needn't come back up the steps, of course. We can walk out to the car through the garden.'

'Ercole, do come,' said Renata, suddenly pleading, as if the short walk were of real significance. 'Ercole.'

He shook his head again. 'It's too much for me,' he said, falling back on his age, falling in with them at last. 'I'm past it.'

'Then don't let's bother at all,' Sophie suggested.

'No, no,' Renata exclaimed, again with disproportionate insistence. 'Of course you must see the fountain. I've seen it many times; I'll stay up here with Ercole.'

'Perhaps another time,' Sophie said.

'My dear, what other time?'

'Yes, go,' the old man said to Sophie. 'You must go. I've seen it, but so long ago – when you come back you must tell me about it. Refresh my memory.'

What a fuss, Tancredi thought again. He moved aside to give Sophie the advantage of the stone banister, and they left the old couple standing at the top of the steps.

In the garden it was warm, and utterly still. 'It's just as well he didn't come,' Sophie remarked as they walked slowly along a narrow pebble path. 'He's got old all at once.'

'No one gets old all at once. . . . No, of course, I understand you – he's suddenly very frail.'

'The first time I visited them in Lucca,' said Sophie, brushing aside long fronds of the shrubbery, 'he took me walking on the walls.' She looked at Tancredi. 'Imagine – we must have walked right around the walls. It's sad to see him like this.'

'Though he still has his wonderful face,' Tancredi said. 'In his day, you know, he was very –' He paused. 'Very charming to women.'

'He is still that,' she said, turning the remark aside.

'Well yes. But I mean –'

She said: 'All Italians are charming to women.'

She said this for politeness, but he thought that perhaps she intended it as a snub, guessing that his life had been rather eventful. He said: 'You mustn't judge that too harshly. You mustn't think it as indiscriminate as it sometimes seems.' She said nothing, knowing that he was accounting for himself, and he went on: 'Petrarch says' (for he often relied on Petrarch to excuse or even ennoble his own behaviour for him) 'it's something to this effect: "Thus, alas, I wander seeking your longed-for self in others." That, of course, is putting it at its best.' He did not know, as he said this, whether he intended Petrarch's little apology as a compliment or an explanation – to her, to his wife, even to Sibilla in her solitary splendour on the coast of Somalia.

They passed on through the arbour draped with a great arch of wisteria, and out once more into the sun. They walked along more slowly still – almost idly, as if they had forgotten the fountain and had no destination.

They came upon it suddenly. It was, as he had said, well placed, in a slightly sunken paved court enclosed by flowering shrubs. The little court was circular and so were the two or three graded steps that formed the base of the fountain. The fountain itself was very old – of thick marble, veined and discoloured. On the shaft and at either side of the basin there were sculptured figures, loosely draped and apparently playing on instruments, from which all detail had been effaced. The bowl of the fountain was shallow and smooth and beautifully whitened, and brimmed with water that poured steadily into it through apertures beneath the figures grouped on either side.

Sophie walked up to the fountain without speaking, and Tancredi came and stood beside her. The basin was at the height of her elbow, and she extended her hand over the rounded edge to dip it in the water, splashing the surrounding marble with ripples of green light.

'How lovely,' she exclaimed. 'Oh, how lovely.'

'Yes, it has its quality,' he agreed. Once again her sudden interest eased his afternoon. 'It has something of its own.'

'Has it always been here?' she asked, still moving her hand in the water, vaguely disrupting the light rushing sound.

He smiled, because she seemed to refer to the beginning of the world. 'Oh yes,' he said, 'I suppose it was in this spot from the beginning. The house in its present form is much later of course.'

Now there was a faint tinkling, and the little gold bracelet she wore slipped over her hand and into the shallow basin of the fountain. It lay there against the worn stone, wavering at them through the water.

'I'll get it for you,' said Tancredi.

'No, no.' She made a motion of putting back his outstretched arm. 'You have your jacket. I can do it more easily.'

She leaned on the whitened outer curve of the fountain, smiling, a little dazzled by the hot sun. She unbuttoned her right cuff and rolled up her sleeve. When her arm was bare above the elbow, she bent over the marble rim and, plunging her hand through the water, brought out the bracelet.

He thought, as he watched her, that in all his life he had never seen a more seductive thing than the unconsidered gesture with which she folded back her sleeve. He saw the brown outer skin of her arm, as she turned her wrist, the surprising vulnerable white of the inward flesh and the veined curve inside the elbow. Her reaching hand and forearm, momentarily transfigured by water, had seemed in that instant to form part of the design – the design attributed to Pisano but probably even older. These simple actions moved him by their involuntary power, their immense accomplishment. He was amazed too by the magnitude of his own response, which gave her gesture real consequence. Although he had spoken to her earlier of his romantic temperament, he was as shaken by this pang of authentic sentiment as if he had encountered a friend totally unchanged after an absence of twenty years.

He recalled how the old man had said to her, at the top of the steps: 'Refresh my memory.'

Holding the wet bracelet, she laughed and looked up at him. The swath of the starched sleeve, standing out from her upper arm, was darkened where it had touched the water. 'How silly,' she said. 'I must have it made tighter – have one of the links removed.'

When he said nothing, she balanced her bare elbow on the stone once more and glanced away. The bracelet was dangling now so loosely from her fingers that it was in danger of falling in again. He reached out and took hold of her arm as if to remove it from the water's edge. She let it rest briefly in his hand. She did not look at him or acknowledge his vision, but for a moment stood still in the sun with her head bowed and her arm, glistening with water, in his grasp, and the little gold chain in her hand.

# Two

'Why are you sitting out here in the dark?' he demanded, coming down the few steps from Signora Brandi's villa and crossing the garden by one of its narrow pebbled paths.

'Oh, Tancredi,' said Luisa Brandi. She stretched out her right hand as he came up and, as he kissed it, included her companion in the greeting with a gesture of her left. 'I think you've met Sophie. At a tea party, she told me.' She paused while he took the more hesitantly extended hand of her niece. 'Pull up that chair and join us. We're waiting for the nightingale.' He scraped the cane chair across the stones. 'Sophie is complaining of the insects, but for my part I like to come out here in the evening. You can hear crickets and owls and, at this time of year, the nightingale. And in any case,' she added, answering him at last, 'it isn't dark.'

It was true; the garden was still coloured with dying light and the surrounding hills retained their features. The side of the villa, terraced on to the hillside and notched with great dark windows, gleamed above them, itself over-hung at the hill's crest by a wood. Briefly extinguished by the house, the wood surged forth again below this formal garden – if formal it could be called with the grass eight inches high and the coloured creepers encircling the arms and legs of the mock-pagan statues and, even more improbably, twined about a row of large cactus. The shaped garden beds, however, were disarmingly well tended and filled with flowers.

'I thought perhaps you had gone away,' said Tancredi, offering his cigarettes, taking one himself and striking a match. 'There were no lights at the front of the house, and no one came when I knocked. In the end, I went round to the kitchen and Isabella let me in.' The flame having almost reached his fingers, he paused to light his cigarette.

'I'm the only one left. They've all gone now, for the summer.' Luisa spoke of her sons and their families, who visited her in the spring and the autumn. 'The house is closed up, except for Isabella and myself. Sometimes Sophie comes up from the town to keep me company in the evenings. Imagine, she comes all this distance and then I bring her out here among the insects. . . . Otherwise I am entirely alone.' Quite without pathos – indeed, with a smile – she repeated: 'Entirely alone.' Turning to Sophie, she went on: 'You see how he makes use of us. We didn't so much as set eyes on him here in the winter. And now, because his friends have gone off to the sea and he has nothing better to do, he comes up here in the evening, beating on our doors. . . . No, no, my dear, I'm only joking. There's no one whose company I enjoy more. As you know.' But he should also know, she thought, that I am perfectly aware of the fact that he came here in the hope of meeting Sophie. Not that they are at all suited to one another, she reflected – and Tancredi has that very beautiful and very troublesome wife, from whom, it seems, he's separated at last. But of course that is what he came for, to see Sophie. I know him so well. 'I've known him since he was a

22

schoolboy,' she said to Sophie. 'Heavens, what a lovely young man he was.'

'People only say that,' Tancredi remarked, 'when they feel that early promise hasn't been fulfilled.'

'Not at all,' returned Luisa, thinking there was truth in what he said. 'I'm sure you have a long history of fulfilled promises.'

'That, for some reason, sounds even worse.'

'Tonight there is the moon,' Sophie said tactfully, and the more unexpectedly because she had her back to the thin crescent that as yet shed no noticeable light.

Luisa leaned back in her garden chair to see the moon through the overhanging branches. Her next remark, how-ever, suggested that her attention had wandered, for she said after a short silence: 'One sees why the ancients hon-oured the laurel; it really is a noble tree.'

They all stared upward into the dark, incisive fronds. Tancredi observed, with the faintly competitive air of someone who has trees of his own, that the tree should be pruned.

Luisa sighed. 'It's what I keep telling Mario' – Mario was the gardener – 'who only says that the shears are broken, as if that took care of everything. He never sug-gests mending them. I would mend them myself, but I'm not good with mechanical things. Oh dear no. In fact, I'm too practical, not ingenious enough. Oh, you can smile' – to Tancredi, who had not waited for this permission – 'but it's true. If I'd been an inventor, I'd have managed to think up the broom, perhaps, or a pair of tongs. Or an umbrella – a stiff one, you know, not the kind that opens and closes.' She laughed suddenly. Sometimes at the end of her quick paragraphs she would pause in this way, with an abrupt flourish, like a skier arrested in a hail of crystal. 'You, Tancredi, are much more ingenious. *Your* umbrella would have opened and shut.'

'And Sophie?' he asked, trying to get the girl to meet his eyes.

'Oh – Sophie, on the other hand, is artistic.'

Sophie smiled to hear on her aunt's lips this dated adjective, which evoked a picture of hand-loomed skirts or ill-proportioned pottery or symmetrical flowers painted on the lids of boxes. She would not look at Tancredi, but she thought more than once that he had come just to see her, and she could not help being pleased. There was something avowed, almost old-fashioned, about his manner of sitting there in her aunt's presence. However, Luisa did not really have the character of a duenna. Her tenderness, while deeply personal, as true tenderness has to be, had a monumental quality as if she saw in one's own need a reflection of all the vulnerability and injustice in the world. Her understanding was too valuable – one could not make trifling claims on it. Sophie thought: They cannot stay for us, precious people; they must go on, for others await them. And I am perfectly able to deal with this man, who does not even attract me (she was sure of this, having given it some thought since she had met him at his sister's), except in so far as he has the qualities that are attractive about Italy itself – grace and the lack of earnestness. He was probably older than he looked. And then there was the language. If I saw him alone, she thought, I would have to wonder all the time about the subjunctive. I don't think I can be bothered.

She hardly says anything, Tancredi was thinking. Facing him in this dusk, with her straight hair and narrow limbs all making long, scarcely curved lines, she was like a delicate, resonant instrument. Her thoughts he imagined to be quite prosaic. Even so, she had some air, however uncertain, of knowledge. At times she seemed to him (as women often did) like a piece of important information he must acquire. He had come to see her and he was pleased simply to be in her presence. Or so he concluded, since he had as yet no sense of wasting his evening.

Possibly, Luisa thought, he should not be allowed to waste Sophie's time. He would not know how to be serious even if circumstances permitted it, and Sophie could not be anything else. For that reason, she was not to be envied, though perhaps in the end she was luckier than he. All at once Luisa felt tired, threatened by a complicated and un-nerving idea, and briefly closed her eyes. When we are young, she thought, we worship romantic love for the wrong reasons, as we do the music of Chopin or the poetry of Keats and, because of that, subsequently repudiate it. Only later, and for quite other reasons, we discover its true importance. And by then it has become tiring even to observe.

'Are you asleep?' Sophie inquired. Luisa had not spoken for so long.

'No, I'm a little tired,' she answered, still with her thoughts. It was now so dark that they could scarcely see one another. 'I was thinking . . .'

'What?'

'Oh – only about Keats. And in that connexion, I really don't think I'm going to wait for this inconsiderate bird.'

'That doesn't sound particularly like Keats,' Sophie said, smiling.

'The connexion was indirect. But I'm getting cold. And I find you were right about the insects.'

'I could bring you a rug,' Tancredi said, rising and putting out his cigarette.

'I think I'm going to bed.' Luisa stood up, although she stayed for a moment by her chair. Sophie got to her feet and Luisa said good night to her, leaning forward to kiss her. 'Of course Tancredi will drive you home,' she said, not at all as a suggestion or as a reminder to him but rather as a pronouncement on the evening. She let Tancredi accompany her through the garden, putting no weight on the hand he placed at her elbow. He walked with unnatural, solicitous slowness, and held aside the branches of the shrubs so that he could stay at her side.

'How sweet it smells,' she remarked. She sighed as they went up the steps to the house, and paused at the top with her hand on one of the open doors.

'What is it?' he asked, alarmed at this exhaustion which he had never seen in her before. 'Are you ill?'

'Just old,' she said. She drew herself up and went inside. The drawing room, lit by one faltering lamp whose bulb had not been thoroughly secured, was high and thick-walled and lined, rather than furnished, with heavy chests, great chairs and tables, and cabinets of books. It was floored with geometrical patterns of large, glossy tiles, and over these Luisa passed, slow and erect, folding her sea-green shawl about her with an invalid's automatic, careful gesture. The hallway was dark, but she crossed it with the confidence of someone who expects no change and was at the foot of the stairs by the time Tancredi found the light switch.

He thought, coming up to her, that she had become very

beautiful in this new state, this old age she attributed to herself. Her strong, almost Oriental features, in this light and beneath the silver coils of her hair, were refined to a supernatural transparency. She had turned on the first step, and stood leaning with one hand on the stair rail, her straight body wrapped in the shawl, which she clasped with the other hand above her waist. He saw that she wanted to mention Sophie but could not bring herself to do so directly.

'Living in this countryside,' she observed, 'if you have foreign friends, is like running a convalescent home. They arrive every summer, pale and nervous, and we get them smoothed out and fattened up. And then send them back to the Front.' Standing this way, on the step, she was slightly taller than he. She wanted to say to him: 'Don't cause her any trouble – let her have her holiday in peace.' Aloud, she added: 'Do you understand?'

'Dear Luisa,' he replied politely. 'It had not even occurred to me that we were behind the lines.'

She laughed and put her hand in his. 'You're very nice, Tancredi,' she said. 'You aren't a rascal, really.'

He could hardly be flattered by this discovery, which had the air of a verdict only arrived at after considerable deliberation. But when she repeated it, almost giving it significance, he said 'No,' simply and seriously, as though he were making an important admission.

She drew away, still with her hand in his. 'How elegant you always are,' she continued more lightly, her eyes wandering over his cream-coloured suit and crisp shirt and his carefully brushed dark hair. 'You wear a new suit almost every day.' She looked into his face. 'Eventually, perhaps, you will find one that is just right for you.'

He stayed at the foot of the stairs and watched her go slowly up. At the landing she stopped again, but merely said: 'Perhaps you would put out the light when I get to the top. Good night, dear Tancredi.'

When the nightingales, one in a cypress and the other hidden in a shrubbery below the garden, began to call to each other, Sophie clasped her hands in her lap and sat up straight, apparently bracing herself for an experience. Across her uplifted head the song passed back and forth – a consummation of the darkness, as if night without this must always be imperfect. She saw Tancredi reappear at the top of the steps and stand for a moment in the light before coming back to her. He made no attempt to soften the sound of his footsteps on the stones as he crossed the garden. He came and sat beside her, in Luisa's chair, but the nightingale, dividing them from the world, divided them also from each other, and they sat listening and remote.

It might be interesting, she thought in her assiduous way, to recall the poem now – how did it go again? (She could scarcely concentrate because the song was insistently beautiful, and she closed her eyes as though the sound might enter there, too.) Ridiculous; she couldn't remember how it started. 'Thou still ...' No, that was the other one. There was that business about Ruth, and then the magic casements. ... But she couldn't for the life of her think of the first line.

Tancredi was thinking of Luisa, whose light he now saw at one of the upper windows and whose shadow moved back and forth within the room. When he was a child his parents had had a summer house at the sea, near Pesaro, and he remembered hearing nightingales in the garden there; he had not, he thought, heard them since – there were fewer of them about perhaps. Luisa then – it was over thirty years ago – would have been a young woman, happy with her husband, bringing up her children in this house, and looking, he imagined, much the same but dark-haired, animated, more easily moved to tears. I would have been in love with her, he realized – and the absolute certainty of this touched him deeply. It struck him like a loss actually suffered, impoverishing his experience, diminishing all his prospects.

To retrieve a reasonable view of things, he looked at once at Sophie, but her face, though very close, was dim and he had lost his earlier sense of her appeal. She offered no intimacy now, sitting there stiff and attentive, as though she were having a lesson. She is not in the least like Luisa, he thought. But the comparison dispirited him and he followed it immediately with the thought that he would make her smile more; she must learn to enjoy things for their own sake. When the nightingale stops, he thought, I will take her hand.

That's it, Sophie thought abruptly, opening her eyes and making a slight movement in her chair. Of course. That's the way it begins – 'My heart aches . . .'

# Three

If he were even five minutes late, she decided, she would leave. And Italians are never punctual; the café, the convenient place to wait, absolves them from that. There is no question of hanging about, no looking lost and unwanted or even disreputable, as there is in hotel lobbies or the foyers of restaurants. One just sits and enjoys the scene, and waits. When he had said to her 'Tomorrow at five,' of course he didn't mean he would be there on the hour. He meant ten past, a quarter past five. She could be gone with a clear conscience by the time he came. He would ask the waiter, and the waiter, understanding everything, would tell him: Yes, the lady was there, stayed a few minutes, and left. If encouraged, the waiter would even describe what she was wearing and whether she had seemed cross when she walked away.

She stopped to buy a newspaper as she went up the slight incline towards the piazza, and she walked on frowning down at the folded headline but scarcely seeing it. She really could not think how she had got herself into this assignation – for that, certainly, was the word for such an appointment with a man one hardly knew. She had kept out of his way – and his way seemed to have coincided with hers to a remarkable degree. But yesterday, meeting by accident in a shop, they had been unexpectedly familiar with one another, leaning on the counter and talking in a light, ready way. He waited while she did her shopping, and they walked out into the street together. Only when she was leaving him had he asked her to see him. 'Tomorrow at five. For a coffee. The big piazza near the post office.' And when she said nothing to this telegraphic invitation, he had shown her, pointing towards the end of the street, precisely the café; its umbrellas could be seen across an open space, beyond a row of leaning houses. 'Will you be all right?' he had asked her then, as he stood at the edge of the sidewalk with his back to the traffic. 'Do you know which way to go?'

She had in truth looked a little lost. She had not known how to refuse him, and she left him almost without a word. For how could she have thought up a polite excuse, standing there in the middle of the street, looking into his face? And in any case the light had changed; she had to cross.

Now, walking up to the café, she felt almost relieved. If they missed each other this afternoon, as they were practically certain to do, he would not try to see her again. She hardly knew him. She could not even remember his last name.

'You're very prompt.' He got up from the little table and pulled out her chair. 'I thought women were always unpunctual.'

And so, in the end, she was annoyed with herself for being on time. However, she smiled and greeted him in an open, almost businesslike way. Let's get this over quickly, her smile said. She sat down beside him and he called the waiter while she looked about the square.

It was a utilitarian piazza in the most modern section of the town. Never having aspired to the magnificence of the town's great central piazza, it had at some stage evidently capitulated completely and agreed to receive the workaday elements of the city's life – the post office, for which the piazza was named, the police station, the main taxi rank, a cinema, and the prim brick headquarters of the local Communist party. All these were nevertheless arranged with an involuntary meridional adroitness, and the general effect was one of space and colour. In the centre of the square (it was, more accurately, a circle haltingly sketched) was a series of flower beds filled with purple and white petunias. The café where they sat was freshly painted, and their corner of it faced the piazza's single architectural asset – a church consecrated to one of the town's numerous patron saints, who appeared in marble above the portico with an open book short-sightedly held before his face.

The transitory polite smile on Sophie's face developed into something less fictitious. The scene was so totally lacking in haste or violence. It provided an easy accustomed setting for the long afternoon, which today had such a monumental afternoon quality that it might have been any afternoon in the whole of memory. It was for just these anonymous public pleasures that Sophie came to Italy. Then, there were times, after all, when one was glad of company – and his was perfectly acceptable. She even recalled his last name.

For Tancredi, it was the time of year when the seasons ceased to have meaning. Now, try as he would, he could not imagine a cold day, a storm, a shower of rain. There were days in winter when the narrow spiralling streets of this town were reduced to slippery channels banked with snow; when, viewed from the foot of its hill, the city rose up like a symmetrical, frosted fir tree, branching into great terraces of church, palace, and piazza. But every spring Tancredi pardoned all this – with true forgiveness, since he could not even remember it. The summer light, the predominant light of the countryside, restored all the true shapes and colours; he got up earlier to enjoy the sight of them. Not that he forgot the complications of his life – the wife he no longer loved, the children from whom he was often separated – but these became more bearable in the light of June. Not that in his office he suffered fools gladly or forgave his enemies – but he was prepared to let them off more lightly than usual. This afternoon he could think of himself, here in the piazza, as a personable man with a woman who did him credit – his vanity was satisfied with an occasional glimpse of this kind. (He would have preferred, perhaps, someone less distraught, more companionable; and if she had belonged to him he would never have let her wear that particular shade of green. However, one could not always have exactly what one liked.)

'What would you like?' he asked her.

The waiter was beside them – looking on, as Sophie had foreseen, with an interest so undisguised that it practically demanded an acknowledgement. She looked at the waiter and then at Tancredi, and they ordered two glasses of vermouth. There seemed to be no pressing necessity to make conversation. It was the most natural thing in the world that they should sit there without speaking, making no attempt to discover one another. Inside the café a popular song was being played on the radio, turned low so that only the highest and loudest notes reached them – and those with a reedy remoteness. Outside, at the table next to theirs, a young couple sat with their little boy, who was

33

eating an ice-cream cone aloud, and their black Pomeranian, which had been tied to the leg of the table. A car circled the piazza, looking for a place to park. A station wagon with a little Swedish flag painted in a corner of the window drew up near the café, and a yellow-haired couple got out, followed by a whole matching set of children.

The immune silence ticked towards its end. Sophie laid her hand on the table.

But he spoke first. 'What would you be doing,' he asked, 'this afternoon? If you had not come to meet me.'

'Oh – I might have stayed at the hotel,' she began vaguely, not bothering to dissemble. 'Written my letters. Or gone to see my aunt.' She cast about for a more satisfactory answer. 'Or taken a walk perhaps.'

'So you see,' he said gravely, 'you're much better off here with me.'

She drank her vermouth, shaking the single wafer of ice round the glass. The radio blurted out the climax of another song. Unsettled, trying to recover the dreamlike afternoon, she stared at the piazza. She was aware of his interest – his curiosity, rather – directed at her so strongly that it could be felt like an element on the exposed parts of her body: on her hands and arms and neck, and her averted eyes.

What a shifty lot they are, these northern women, he was thinking, amused. Always afraid you might find them interesting or treat them as something other than men. There are really only two kinds – they are either strident or repressed. It's the way they're brought up; they can't help themselves. 'I wonder if you would help me,' he began, and paused maliciously to see how much her apprehension would increase.

But she was quite composed. 'Of course,' she said. 'If I can.'

'I have to buy a frame for a painting. The shop isn't far from here. Perhaps you would come and help me choose.'

'Certainly,' she said. 'Though I know nothing about it.' She drank again. Across the café the Swedes had joined two tables together. Three little girls in blue dresses sat up eating *gelati* and swinging their legs, and a tiny boy in a sailor suit sipped inattentively from a spoon presented by his mother. The father, like the marble saint on the far side of the piazza, held an open book close to his eyes. They took turns at talking, loudly and gaily, in their quick lilting voices.

'There are only two kinds of Swedes,' Sophie remarked, watching them. 'Fearful bores or very nice.'

Tancredi counted out some change on to the table. 'Those are the only kinds there are of any people,' he said. He finished his vermouth, which until then he had not touched, in a single gulp. 'But these generalizations are always false in any case.'

The shop was at the foot of a short street leading down from the piazza. It was a prosperous place, fronted by a double window filled with *cornici* and with various examples of coloured shutters that were also sold there. There was a small ceremony of receiving Tancredi. The owner was called from the back of the premises, shook hands, and spoke at length about his family and his new car. A space was made for Sophie to put her handbag on the dusty counter.

'Plain gold,' Tancredi said, 'and quite narrow.' The samples dangled in long rows on the wall, and he began handling them. 'No, this is too flat. And this too broad.'

'This, Professore?'

'No – something simple.'

'What about this?' She held it out to him, and he came over to look.

'What an eye you have – absolutely perfect. How did you find it? This is just what I want.' He called to the boy behind the counter. Sophie went to sit on a rickety chair while he stood waiting, fingering the slips of gilded wood. When the boy came with his block and pencil, however, she noticed that he ordered a frame slightly different from the one she had suggested. 'You'll send someone up to my sister's house then?' he said to the boy.

'Yes, Professore.'

'When?'

'Tomorrow, at this time?'

'No. No, you'd better come in the morning. Early, before I leave for my office.'

Sophie, faintly irritated, stood up and brushed at her handbag with the edge of her newspaper.

When they were out in the street again, he asked her: 'Where would you like to go? Shall we go for a drive?'

She said: 'I'm afraid I must go home.'

'Home? Why must you go home?'

She found herself once more on a busy sidewalk with him, looking into his face. She was on the downward side of the steep slope and had an awkward sensation of confronting him. She said with more resolution: 'I mean that I *want* to go home.'

'You'll come tomorrow?'

'Oh no,' she said.

'The letters,' he said with a smile. 'The walks. Your aunt.'

She began to walk slowly on, at his side, up the slope toward the piazza. 'I can't,' she said.

'Nevertheless, I'll look for you in the piazza. At five?' His head was turned to her as they walked. 'Think of me – as another possibility, along with the letters and the walks. A sort of aunt perhaps.' He was not quite laughing, for he wanted to be sure before he left her that she would come. At the top of the street he took her hand and let her say good-bye. He did not watch her walk away, but strolled off across the piazza with his hands in his pockets.

# Four

One day late in June when the flat modern clock outside the post office said ten past five, Sophie began to look up from her postcards, sending unconcerned glances around the piazza in search of his light-coloured suit and dark head; turning, just as unconcerned, to see if the navy-blue car had arrived in the parking area. 'I miss you all,' she was writing, on the back of a Last Judgment, when his shadow fell on the half-inscribed card and his hand on her lifted wrist. She looked up, this time into his eyes.

'Don't let me interrupt you,' he said, sitting beside her and still lightly grasping her hand – her right hand, with the pen in it.

She greeted him, unsmiling, happy. 'I was wondering if you'd come.'

'Was that why you looked so strange? But, my dear girl, I'm not late, you know.'

'Not really, no. It's just that I have a thing about waiting.'

He frowned. 'A thing? What thing?'

'I only mean I hate to wait. It's a state of emergency – everything becomes so concentrated.'

'You'll get over that,' he remarked, releasing her hand and looking over her head for the waiter.

'When?' she asked, amused to think there were habits she might still grow out of.

He looked back into her face. 'When you realize that I will always come.' The waiter arrived, but instead of ordering Tancredi paid him for her coffee and sent him away. 'Let's go – I have the car over there.'

On her postcard she added: 'But I am happy here.' She fixed the last stamp to it and put it away with the others in her handbag. She knew she need not hurry to please him; he would be pleased whatever she did. She stood up and smoothed her dress. When they left the thin shade of the umbrella she put up a hand to protect her eyes. Not until they were sitting in the car did she ask: 'Where are we going?'

'Let's get out of the town and then see.' He swung the car around, leaning out to tip the shabby parking attendant. 'It won't be as hot as this once we're moving.'

He drove slowly down the town's main street, which was narrow, cobbled, lined with steep handsome buildings and filled with pedestrians and little cars. The shadows from the buildings were red or dark gold. Groups of girls walked with their arms about each other's waists. Friends, meeting in the middle of the street, stayed there to talk. Several people greeted Tancredi, and one or two leaned in at the window to exchange a few words. There was none of the usual swift anonymity of a drive through a town – this ride had rather the character of a slow progress in an open carriage.

'In the Middle Ages,' Tancredi said, 'there was nothing but foot traffic in these streets. Pregnant women were allowed to ride on donkeys, but even then someone had to walk before them calling out a warning. The streets were never meant to bear this kind of traffic – look how the paving has sunk.' He waved briefly to an elderly man in a white suit and then to a young couple. 'It'll be easier when we get beyond the Duomo.'

Within a few minutes they passed the turn-off leading to the cathedral and moved along more quickly until at last they drove under the crenelated arches of an immense double gate.

They might have stepped from a busy house into a garden. The city fell behind them – the encumbered streets, the impeded drive, the glances and voices, all the peculiar suspense of towns. The stillness into which they drove was the more impressive – one might almost have said the more reproachful – for its imminence. It pressed, along with the caper and the climbing roses, upon the city's outer walls.

In this part of Italy the harvest begins early. By midsummer the whole countryside is bare and multitudes of small hills, more shapely than ever in their exposure, have turned to dry gold. The grain is variously stacked, according to the district – sometimes propped in circular, tentlike patterns, sometimes rounded like a series of mosques, here standing austerely, in keeping with the local architecture, in tall indented loaves. Coming so early, the harvest seems to lie at the heart of summer rather than to announce its overthrow. The harvesters' suppers are truly celebrations and not – like the later wine festivals – overshadowed by the autumn.

'This is the main road,' he said. 'The road for Rome. We'll turn off in a minute.'

But it was several minutes before they left the road. They climbed then, over a narrow track of stones and white dust, between low-slung fences of staked vines and tough, stunted olive trees. Pebbles were flung up noisily about the wheels, and behind the car the dust emerged in a languid cloud. The sky, though always water-colour, was a bright bright blue – an injudicious paint-box azure, distantly reflected violet in the farthest uplands.

They jolted slowly over this crest of the fields. Sophie brought a scarf out of her handbag and tied it round her hair. When they came to the highest rise, Tancredi had to pull aside to let a loaded truck pass by. He stopped the car in a slight depression below the road, and they smiled to three sunburned workmen sitting on slabs of the quarried stone with which the truck was loaded. A boy perched at the back waved to Sophie and called out: 'Ca . . . rina.'

Tancredi drove the car back on to the road. A few yards farther on he stopped again and turned off the engine. Sophie lowered her window, which she had closed against the dust raised by the truck, and a slight breeze blew across them.

'Shall we walk a little way?' he asked, turning his head from the view.

She opened her door, which swung back heavily from the car's angle, but before she could get out he had come round to help her. The stubble at the field's edge scraped about the straps of her sandals as she stepped down. They walked along the side of the road, ahead of the car. Dust and the little stones of the road found their way between her toes. She had left her purse in the car and, like an adolescent, did not know what to do with her hands. Less solicitous than before, he walked at her side and looked about him.

Here the corn had not been gathered, and lay in loose

bundles in the fields. Endless golden hills were posted with clusters or straight lines of black cypresses and sometimes, magnificently, with one splendid tree. A handful of co-operative farmhouses, painted white, faced them on an approaching hillside, but the few other buildings were isolated, ancient, and of grey stone. From the fields the scents were of the dry red earth and the cut grain and of rosemary.

Tancredi's feelings, stirred to an easy Latin intensity, rushed forth to greet the landscape. Although he had been born and brought up far to the south, this countryside was to him phenomenal, possessed of an almost communicable significance. They walked along in silence until she paused to shake a stone from her shoe. Then he stood still and, when she looked up, said to her: 'We've come at the right moment – the light is so beautiful.' He spoke in a lowered voice, as if the hills were a flock of birds that might get up and fly away.

'Yes, lovely,' she replied, in an abstracted, mechanical voice, glancing towards the horizon as she walked on.

The scene might have been of Tancredi's own creation, so keen was his disappointment. He watched her with injured pride at such ingratitude, like a chef with whose great dish a diner only toys. And yet, it was this very lack of sympathy, in a person obviously responsive, that attracted him; and even now he wondered how, and if ever, he might tap the spring of a passion sometimes discernible in her expression and gestures.

If the walk had aroused any emotion in Sophie, it was the solitary pang of the expatriate. This countryside – which usually pretended to be exclusively decorative, which posed for paintings and photographs, feigned a private income – was now revealed to her in all its true domestic purpose. She felt like an outsider at a family feast. She wondered: What am I doing here, on this road, with this man, these sights, this language? She wished she were an authentic tourist – an Englishman come to flaunt his reticence, an American secretly hankering for gift wrapping and matching towels. She did not really know where she most belonged. Even those places to which she felt most drawn were mere approximations of home.

'Let's go back,' she said suddenly, turning to him, seeing him across this gulf.

He had recovered his good humour. He stood still again and smiled at her. 'You are always wanting to go home,' he said, and took her lightly by the wrists as if he would detain her.

Her empty hands struggled under the tightening grasp. She experienced a fleeting, irrational terror of a strength superior to her own. When he leaned forward to kiss her, she stepped back awkwardly on the uneven road and said in a high, unnerved voice: 'No. I don't want to.' It was not simply that she did not want his kiss. She did not want this inadvertent, troublesome encounter. She did not want to be disturbed.

After a second or two he released her, spreading his hands open in an attitude almost identical to her own. Her scarf had slipped back across her shoulders and her hair fell forward on her cheeks and brow. He stared at her. 'Let's go then,' he agreed, pained as he had been over her indifference to the landscape. There is no pleasing her, he thought.

He helped her into the car and, with a little difficulty, started the engine. The anger he was too proud to inflict

43

on her showed in his treatment of the car. The motor roared, he wrenched the wheel around, trying absurdly to turn in one attempt. The turn eventually completed, they pitched forward down the rough road. But when they reached the highway, he slowed again to enter the traffic, and asked her in a perfectly controlled voice where she would like to be taken.

'To the hotel,' she told him, her voice less easy than his. Her behaviour, since he manifestly thought it so, seemed to her cold and unaccountable. After all, she reasoned with herself, if I have coffee with him occasionally, does that give him the right to make love to me? (But this she knew to be unjust; his right to approach her was implicit in all their meetings.) She thought: It isn't that I am un-approachable; it is the circumstances. She said, and her voice was thin and shaken as it had been when they stood on the road: 'I can't see you any more.'

After a silence he said carefully: 'Why is that?' and she was touched by the serious inquiry in his voice, as if he found the matter more crucial than anger.

'It must be obvious.' She too was more earnest, looking at him swiftly, affirming her position by clasping her hands in her lap. His idea of her, she thought, was as superficial as her own impression of this countryside: he saw her on holiday, and not as she actually was – someone with parents, bills, ailments, someone who did the shopping and went to the dentist and was accountable to friends.

'I'll be in the piazza tomorrow,' he said – but without confidence, for the first time.

'Please,' she said. 'I won't come.'

The walls of the town were in sight over the slope of the road. He asked her: 'Is this because I tried to kiss you?'

'No.' And for the first time she searched her thoughts to give him an honest reply. 'It's because, if things had been different, I would have let you.' The fields dropped away, and they entered the city by the Roman Gate.

# Five

Sophie was going out to lunch. It had been arranged that Luisa, with two friends, would call for her at the hotel and take her to lunch at a restaurant in the town. Although she went to some trouble over her appearance and was not ready at the appointed time, the three others were later still. She came downstairs and sat on a sofa at the back of the lobby, where long windows overlooked a garden. Below her, in bright morning sun, the plants and flowers flashed with an almost tropical prodigality; beneath her feet, the same flowers, shaded lilac by the overhanging folds of her dress, were perpetuated in faintly crazed tiles. She leaned back and crossed her legs. She sighed.

'You make a pretty picture,' her aunt said, appearing at her side. 'We'd better not sit down. We're so late already – my fault of course – and we have a reservation. You know Daria. And this is Massimo Tordini.'

Sophie smiled to a tall woman dressed in white, with an enclosed pale face and a dome of teased golden hair. She gave her hand to Tordini, who was at once squat and dapper, a retired musician visiting the town's summer arts festival. He held her hand, then kissed it, paid her an extravagant compliment, and reminded Luisa that he had left his car in a forbidden space. They walked back slowly through the hotel lobby in pairs. Daria, incredibly, had brought a white spiked parasol, which aloofly pecked the patterned tiles at every step. With this, and her high insubstantial hair, she was as self-possessed, as perfectly balanced as Queen Mary. Luisa walked with her, on the opposite side from the parasol – letting her have, as it were, her sword arm free.

Walking behind with Tordini, Sophie contrasted Daria's figure with her aunt's. Luisa's body was also straight and disciplined, but somehow more yielding, more ready to stoop, its pride more intelligible. Her aunt's grey head was inclined towards Daria's and she was laughing.

Tordini detained Sophie with a finger on her arm. 'Someone wants you.'

They had reached the door of the hotel, and she turned to find a lame young man from the Reception at her side, with an envelope in his hand.

'It just came for you,' he said. 'An *espresso*.'

She took it from him and held it in both her hands, looking at the postmark. Tordini pulled back the heavy glass door and they passed out into the street.

'You have a letter,' Daria observed unnecessarily.

'A special-delivery,' remarked Luisa.

Sophie screwed up her eyes in the fierce sunlight, still frowning at the envelope. She felt the two women looking at her. 'It's from Grosseto,' she said. 'I don't know anyone at Grosseto.' She turned it over to open it and saw the name on the back. I had never even seen his handwriting, she thought.

Daria sat in the front seat of the car with Tordini. Sophie, in the back with Luisa, laid the unopened envelope on her knee. She resisted pleasure, as for days she had resisted sadness. She pretended to herself that she was Daria, blank, erect, armoured in white silk.

'Massimo,' Luisa complained, 'this car is like a furnace.'

'We have hardly any distance to go,' he said. 'Can I turn down here – is this a one-way street?' A shriek of horns assured him that it was. 'Keep an eye out for a parking place.'

In the end they parked beside the restaurant, in another forbidden spot. The interior of the restaurant was cool; its thick red walls and low, curved ceiling gave a sense of being underground. They had a table in a corner and Daria laid her parasol on the floor since, despite repeated attempts, it could not be made to stand against the wall.

'It will get dirty,' said Luisa.

Sophie said: 'Will you forgive me if I open my letter?'

'Of course, dear. I can't imagine how you've waited so long.'

'It's nylon,' said Daria. She was speaking of her parasol.

Sophie slit the envelope with her finger and drew out a single sheet written on both sides.

'It must be a love letter,' Tordini said, teasing her.

'My sweet Sophie,' the letter began, 'This is not a love letter.'

'Of course it is,' Luisa agreed.

'Have you thought about what you want?' Tordini waved to the waiter. 'We're ready to order. What's good today? Is the fish fresh?'

Sophie read on. 'I went to the piazza, as I said I would. I find that I too have A Thing about waiting, when it is for you and you don't come. . . . On Friday I drove to the coast –'

'Sophie, will you have *antipasto*? Two then. And red or white?'

'– to visit my children, and I am spending the night here at Grosseto on business on the way back. If you will see me when I return, please send a note to my house tomorrow.'

She folded the page in two without finishing it, and laid it beside her plate. The concluding lines of the letter, written in a more impetuous hand, started up from the white cloth between her plate and her wineglass, but she could scarcely decipher them: '. . . explain myself . . . if you were made of flesh instead of air.'

Tordini said: 'It's strange that love letters' – he had forgotten how the subject had come up – 'to the Anglo-Saxon mind always take on the character of ravings.'

'Unless they are very understated,' Luisa agreed.

Sophie sipped her wine. Her eye fell again on the fold of the letter. '*Se invece che d'aria tu fossi di carne.*' It's well phrased, she thought – like a line from a libretto.

'But I suppose,' Tordini went on, 'that kind of language *is* pretty appalling, if you take it seriously.'

'Anything's appalling,' said Luisa, 'if you take it seriously.'

Sophie ate an olive from her *antipasto* and a slice of ham. Of course, she thought, I can't see him. Of course I can't. She smiled at Tordini, who had started telling jokes. Only – why should I mind as much as this? She felt, for their meetings in the piazza, an exquisite nostalgia, as if they had belonged to a distant idyll in a country never to be revisited.

Tordini was saying, his hands spread open before him: 'And then this Italian says to his friend: "Why are you

49

always with foreign girls? What is it they do that's so special, these foreign girls?" ' The waiter took away his plate and put down the dish of pasta. 'Thank you. And the friend replies: "*They leave.*" '

Sophie laughed. For a moment she thought: I am going to cry. No, I can't cry here. Only children cry in public. It's the sort of thing one should do in childhood, quickly, before it's too late. The events of the morning rocked before her – the blaze of flowers by the hotel window, Daria spiking the coloured tiles with her parasol at every step. Perhaps I have a touch of the sun, she wondered. Or too much wine. And then she thought sharply: I won't see him. She shifted her foot determinedly beneath the table.

'I'm so sorry,' she said to Daria. 'I trod on your sunshade.'

# Six

A boy with a handcart was selling carnations. They were only one hundred lire a bunch, according to the sign, and didn't look in the least wilted.

'How large is a bunch?' Sophie asked him. He held it up for her, the flowers wobbling on their long, supple stems. 'Two pink then. And one of the deep red.'

He wrapped the ends in newspaper and she paid him, holding the sheaf of flowers awkwardly on her arm and counting out the coins. He put the money in a black cloth bag. 'It's a beautiful day,' he said.

'Oh yes.' She smiled, and shifted the carnations into the crook of her arm. How absurd, she thought, to have bought these flowers; now I have to go home and put them in water. And she began to climb the steep street she had just come down. The stems in their damp paper rested against her body, and the strong delicious scent rose over her face. But they *are* lovely, she thought, and they'll last until I go.

Her way back to the hotel lay past the post office. She crossed the wide, unshaded piazza without a glance at the café, although it was early in the afternoon and in any case she knew he wouldn't be there. It was two days since she had received his letter. In another two days she would be gone. Except for the possibility of such an accident – running into him in the street or the piazza – she need never meet him again. It was for this reason, perhaps, that she imagined she saw him so many times as she walked down the main street of the town.

Yet, oddly, as she strolled along, she thought of Tancredi only indirectly. She was thinking, rather, of a man she had loved when she was a schoolgirl, and she saw herself walking up and down with him in a garden, anxiously listening to his complicated exposition of the reasons why he could not love her in return. It must be the carnations, she thought suddenly – the smell of the carnations – that brought that far-off garden and that other summer into her mind. She had not thought of it for years, and was glad now to be reminded of the intricate, lasting nature of any form of love.

The entrance of the hotel was beautifully cool after her walk through the streets. She went over to the desk for her key, but the young man at the Reception came limping out to meet her. He thought she did not understand what he said to her, and repeated his message, directing her to the back of the lobby with his hand.

Tancredi had seen her first, and in the instant before their eyes met he had a strong impression of her appearance. He thought involuntarily (as he sometimes thought if he saw a stylish woman walking alone in the evening or a girl leaning out of a window): She is in love. So detached was this judgement that his first response to it was a pang of jealousy.

He stood up as she came across the coloured tiles to where he was waiting by the windows. She made a movement to put the flowers from her, as if they gave her an unfair advantage. He took them gently out of her grasp and, calling one of the bellboys, asked for them to be put into water. She made no attempt to give him her hand or to speak casually. She came and sat beside him on the sofa with her head slightly lowered and her hands in her lap.

'Don't be annoyed,' he said.

'I'm going away soon.'

'Because of me?'

She glanced up and half smiled. 'You're a threat to me.'

He said seriously: 'You must forgive me for that.'

'You don't deny it,' she observed.

'Are you always like this?'

'Like what?'

'Following the score instead of listening to the music?'

She shook her head, but not in answer to his question. He lifted her hand on to his knee and laid his own hand over it. 'You won't leave,' he said.

She stayed in her slack, acquiescent attitude – like a defeated general, not accounting for the errors that led to this predicament.

He said: 'You aren't happy now. But I promise that you will be.' When he removed his hand, hers remained on his knee as though she had placed it there to comfort him. 'Tomorrow,' he said.

Tomorrow seemed to her as remote, as unlikely as the end of the summer. She thought that probably she would not go away after all; they could have their afternoons again, for a while, in the piazza. Nothing need be undone; nothing more need happen. She thought that, since he said so, perhaps she would be happy.

'Tomorrow,' he said, 'we can make some plans.'

She looked up at him. 'Plans?'

'It would be better,' he said, 'not to go on meeting in the piazza.'

She sat up straight. Their heads, which had been almost touching, now parted. She moved her hand back into her lap. And the bellboy, who had been hesitating in the middle of the lobby, seized the opportunity to come up with her flowers in a brass vase.

# Seven

In this town every summer a festival is held to celebrate an ancient battle – to celebrate the battle rather than the victory, which was gained by the opposing side. It was, in fact, a decisive victory, a turning point in the town's brief but illustrious medieval prominence. But the men of the town conducted themselves so valiantly in the field, under so gallant a commander (Guelph or Ghibelline, it is not easily established), and the defeat was in all its aspects so utterly conclusive, that its celebration each year has become one of the town's, and the nation's, greatest spectacles.

During the festival the town can be entered only on foot. Empty cars and buses stand along the roads outside the walls, and even in the fields. At the railway station, which is beyond the main gate, special trains deliver tourists and visitors for a week beforehand, and in the town itself every hotel and *pensione* is full to bursting and every spare room is let. In the vast main piazza each window is draped with tawny or crimson cloth, and on the night of the festival the campanile of the Palazzo Pubblico is lighted from top to bottom with flares. The main streets are decorated with embroidered banners and with the shields and devices of the city's saints and heroes. (These personages originate without exception in the Middle Ages; in fact, it is said of this town that when its citizens speak of 'the turn of the century', they mean the fourteenth century. In 1944, when the retreating German front approached the city walls with the Allies in close pursuit, the townspeople closed the gates – with some mechanical difficulty, since this had last been done in 1416.)

The festival takes the form of a procession, through the streets and into the piazza, of the members of the city's ancient guilds. The trades that the guilds represent have mostly become obsolete and the guilds have long since been translated into associations comprising various factions of the town. These factions command a fanatical loyalty within their own ranks and maintain bitter opposition towards one another. The Halberd Makers are so irrevocably set against the Embroiderers and Weavers, and so on throughout twenty guilds, that marriage into another guild is unthinkable to a truly staunch member. At the time of the festival, when feeling is at its peak, it becomes dangerous for the members of one society to appear in the domain of another.

The procession takes several hours to pass through the city to the main square. It moves in solemn silence except for an occasional flourish of silver trumpets or a roll of drums, and the steady, portentous tolling of the bell in the campanile. The members of the guilds wear rich medieval costume, silks and velvets heavily embroidered in clear, flashing colours; a few dignitaries appear in helmet and breastplate and on horseback, the horses also hooded and heavily accoutred. Arriving in the square, the guilds present their banners to the assembled nobles of the town – a collection of tremulous elderly gentlemen bearing certain of the proudest and most infamous names in European history. In the evening the guilds disperse through the town in order to work off their heightened animosities. Feuding families reaffirm mutual antagonism, duels are fought, blows exchanged, and occasionally a life taken.

The festival is one of the most splendid sights in Italy. It may also be said to reproduce in miniature all the rancour and intolerance of the world.

The preparations for this festival had completely disrupted the simple routine of Sophie's day. The courteous, fatalistic character of the town was now transfigured into something clamorous and obsessive. She was continually being offered, at the hairdresser or the money-changer, even in the hotel, a ticket for a window along the route of the procession, or a knot of coloured ribbon which would indicate her sympathies for a particular guild. The central piazza had been filled with rickety wooden stands that would seat leading citizens of the town during the ceremony of the banners, and it could scarcely be entered, much less crossed. The main streets, though empty of traffic, were filled with little men carrying large planks or trestles and were sometimes barricaded for a rehearsal. In the churches there were special services to bless the respective guilds. Sophie, who loathed public spectacles but thought it priggish to say so, was drawn along in this meaningless drama like someone who, lacking the strength of will to become a conscientious objector, reluctantly participates in a war.

Tancredi, himself something of a deserter in this annual conflict, had gone to the coast again to visit his children.

This year he would willingly have stayed in the town because of Sophie; instead, because of her, he found himself at the sea.

Sophie in these past two weeks had been both submissive and withdrawn – greeting him, when he came to see her each afternoon, with an intense, confiding pleasure, then relapsing into apprehensive silence or listening too attentively to his idlest remark. He understood, or thought he understood, that she felt herself in some way committed and that this was for her a means merely of gaining time. He patiently came to her every day and on weekends took her for long drives during which he talked a great deal or – what was to him more alien – sat for long intervals in silence, her wrist beneath his unavoided hand. He drove her all over the surrounding countryside. They admired the natural beauty of the landscape and the architecture of the towns; they climbed the towers, stared at the pictures, criticized the dim light in the churches and the steepness of the ubiquitous steps. He was pleased to be in these beautiful places, which he had known all his adult life, with someone who gave them a new sense of being enjoyed. It was only in the car, alone with him, that she became subdued and melancholy. Once, after a particularly pleasant afternoon at Cortona, she burst into tears. His forthright Italian sensuality found her behaviour neurotic and absurd. Nevertheless he accepted it, and was surprised by his own forbearance. He saw that she was apprehensive, not of what she must prevent but of what she knew must occur. And for this reason, when she urged him to go to the sea as he had planned to do, he at last agreed.

Sophie herself thought that she desperately wanted him to go. Now, in his company, she was like a traveller who stands one morning on the deck of a ship in a strange harbour, studying the country where she is to live; who wonders which of these grouped houses is to grow familiar, which of these streets most travelled, whether those parks, so attractive in the early sunshine, will become perhaps sinister by night. She did not even ask herself: Where will it lead? – assuming that she could only come, as it were, to grief. His awareness of this, his disarming, undemanding kindness, could not reassure her. Such reassurance is not within anyone's power. Someone who says 'Trust me' must always hope in his heart that you will keep something in reserve; 'Never leave me' can only represent an inquiry into present intentions.

And so Tancredi went for a week to the sea and Sophie stayed for the festival.

On the morning of the actual day a ceremony was held in the Duomo. On the floor of the cathedral a famous series of Biblical scenes in marble inlay was annually uncovered for the occasion – it was protected by wooden boards during the rest of the year. Sophie, who had never seen this floor, found it impossible to get into the church, and waited outside in the hot sun for the crowd to disperse after the ceremony. Even so, when she eventually got inside she had only glimpses of the inlaid scenes; the most fragile areas were roped off with twists of scarlet silk and the remainder lost beneath her own feet and other people's. The crowd – of townspeople, children, and tourists – was so dense in the cathedral that she could not get back to the main door and finally found her way into the baptistery and out through a small domestic door there. This led on to a flight of long marble steps, which in turn descended into one of the busiest streets of the town.

Sophie sat down on one of the worn steps, solitary, above the street, and watched the crowd. Everyone wore their best clothes – the girls in crisp cottons, the women in demure silk or linen suits. The men also wore light colours, their white shirts open at the neck, their jackets thrown across one shoulder. There were children everywhere, only slightly cowed by their best clothes and their mothers' constant injunctions. The little men of the trestles and the barricades still pressed through the crowd. Of much greater consequence were occasional figures in gold or scarlet – members of the procession already in costume. These were mostly young men wearing dark fringed wigs and exalted expressions, and they made their way through the crowd easily enough, since it fell back respectfully before them. They were impressive, these young men, in the magnificence of their regalia, the centuries of inter-breeding reflected in their lean, haughty faces. And for the style, the very conviction that they brought to their non-sensical rites.

Except for these melodramatic interruptions, the crowd passed steadily back and forth. From time to time some-one, glancing upward, stared curiously at an unexpected detail – the foreign-looking woman in print dress, sun-glasses, and sandals, her elbows on her knees and her chin in her hands – on the otherwise deserted steps of the bap-tistery. The curiosity, however, was brief; the crowd, en-grossed, had no real interest in her judgement.

When she could stand the sun no longer, she got to her feet and went down into the crowd. By now the press of people was sorting itself out, going home for an early lunch in order to be in time for the procession, which started at three. The young men in costume had all disappeared. Sophie wound her way slowly among families and around lovers and reached the main street and her hotel.

'You'll be going out to the procession?' said the lame young man who gave her her key. His certainty made it unnecessary for her to do more than smile. There was a note from Luisa: 'If you want a refuge from the festival, come out to the house whenever you like.'

She went to her room. The shutters had been closed, and she lay down on her bed in the dark. She would not see the procession. She would not go to her aunt's villa. She would lie on her bed in the dark. She missed Tancredi.

She was awakened by the slow tolling of a bell. It was the great bell in the campanile announcing the opening of the festival. It would toll all afternoon while the guilds made their way through the streets of the town. Now the whole city was crammed along sidewalks, into doorways, on to balconies and ledges, even on top of roofs, to watch the spectacle. The silver trumpets were blown, and blown again. The drums rolled. The procession must now be appearing in the main street. No one would applaud or speak; no one (and this in Italy!) would call out: 'There's our Giuseppe!' or 'Bravo, Tonino!' First would come the trumpeters, and small boys with kettledrums; then, at some distance, the officers of the guild, on horseback; and on foot the lesser representatives, all magnificent in array, austere in expression, unshakeable in purposelessness. A cross would be carried, and a likeness – if such it may be called – of the Virgin. And ancient weapons such as one sees in the Tower of London, here glittering as if they went in constant expectation of use.

Sophie got up and stood by the window. Her room at

the hotel looked down a hillside, over the city walls and on the countryside. She had no reason to suppose that the festival would have made a change in the scene – and there was none. Only, as she opened the shutters, the bell boomed louder, widening into the room. She leaned her head against the window frame. One may not in the least want to see a festival; one may think it foolish, infantile, a great nuisance. Nevertheless, one may not wish to be the only person in the world not attending it.

How can a telephone bell, even when it rings, miraculously, from a distance of one hundred kilometres, compete with the tolling of a colossal ceremonial bell that has been rung at measured intervals, for momentous occasions, during the last eight centuries? The telephone, a device of wires and plastic, cannot hope to sound other than ephemeral, bleating into the bronze face of history. And this being the case, why should such a negligible sound have excited a greater response than the inexorable voice proclaiming from the campanile? For Sophie even closed the shutters, hastily, to muffle the tolling of the bell before she crossed the room; even pressed her hand to her exposed ear, to shut out the voice of authority as she picked up the receiver and spoke.

'Can you hear me?'

She sat down on the bed. She smiled. 'Only just. There's this blasted bell. Where are you?'

'At Port Santo Stefano.'

'Whatever are you doing there?'

'I'm on the way to Florence to see my lawyer.' There was a long silence, eventually interrupted by the operator, who thought the call was finished. 'We are talking,' said Tancredi inaccurately. They were silent again.

He said: 'I have to tell you something. Don't be horrified.' She still said nothing and he went straight on. 'I'm in love with you.'

There was another long pause. At last she said: 'You have a funny idea of what's horrifying.'

'I could reach you by this evening. Would you come to Florence with me?'

'Yes,' she said.

'That damned festival – I won't be able to come into the city.' He paused again, calculating. 'I can be there, outside the main gate, by eight o'clock. Can you get to the railway station? I'll pick you up outside the station.'

'But we'd never reach Florence tonight.'

'No. We'd have to stop somewhere along the way and go on tomorrow.'

She pressed her free hand more closely to her ear, but he said nothing more. 'Be careful on the road,' she said.

When she replaced the receiver (the telephone gave a few shattering terminal cries), she lay down again on the bed. The apprehension of these last weeks with him resolved itself into a series of practical concerns, and she occupied herself with these as though there were nothing else to be considered. Money, her passport, clothes she would need for a day or two, a sweater for the drive; nothing heavy, since she must cross the town on foot this evening to get to the gate. She would allow herself half an hour for the walk – a little more perhaps. The procession would be over at seven, the participants and the crowd dispersed. Half an hour would be plenty. . . . She felt not as if she had taken a decision but as though she had now relinquished any possibility of doing so. She slept.

She walked out of the hotel in the evening carrying one

small bag. At first the streets were almost empty, although a scattering of papers testified to the passing of the crowd. A few straggling spectators, mostly in family groups, were making their way home. But when she approached the piazza, the crowd became suddenly thicker until, in the main street, she could scarcely move against it. She was, as far as she could see, the only person in the entire town going in this particular direction. The press of people surged upon her with a frantic disregard, shouting, jostling, careering along – one would almost have thought, in flight. Sophie, frightened, drew back against the wall to let the commotion pass by. Strained, excited faces flashed into hers, insistent cries deafened her; a woman or a child was screaming, caught in the irresistible advance.

There came an interruption in the rush of people – who, Sophie realized, were only now dispersing from the piazza. Abruptly, terrifyingly, the way ahead was filled with the blue-and-crimson costumes of one of the guilds, and the young men of the procession strode into the wake of the retreating crowd. They were not now in the perfect order of the procession but pushed one another, shoulder to shoulder in a close group, like a clan of marauding youths. The coarse hair of their wigs, black and sometimes auburn, squarely swept their shoulders. Some had taken off the cushion-like velvet caps they wore and carried them in their hands, the long plumes reaching the ground. Others rested their hands on wooden swords or daggers fixed at their sides. They spoke – not hysterically like the crowd but tersely, among themselves, savouring the awe of the spectators but detached from it.

Pushing her way along beside the wall, Sophie managed to get to a corner and turn down another street. This was the street she had come through that morning from the Duomo, and she reached the foot of the litter-strewn but empty steps leading up to the baptistery. The crowd here seemed penetrable, and she was about to pass the foot of the steps when there was a sharp roll of drums and another of the guilds, this time in gold and black, appeared in the street before her. In this group there were horsemen. The horses pranced nervously and reared at the drums. The crowd, shrieking, began to run. Sophie climbed up two or three steps. Standing there above the crowd, she could see that the street ahead was completely blocked.

Panic now rose into her own throat. It was after seven-thirty. She thought in despair: I will never get through this. Never. I'll have to walk right round the walls – it will take me hours.

She remembered then the side door into the baptistery. It was getting dark, and she went up the steps unnoticed and put her hand against the little wooden door. It was open, perhaps through an oversight, and she went inside, into the dim, cold marble silence of the baptistery, and passed through to the transept of the cathedral.

Intimidated, she stopped. She stood resting one hand against the fluting of a huge column and looked down the dark empty church. The nave, cleared for the ceremony that morning, was marked only by its double row of colossal pillars and by the banners that projected from them on thick gilt rods. The fading daylight came, greatly diminished, through high and very narrow windows and from a circular window above the altar. The smell of incense and age, the smell of religion itself, was lightless. She began to walk down the centre aisle. Her sandalled feet, on the precious paving that had been obscured from her view that morning and was now once more almost indistinguishable, made a light ringing sound that echoed up into the roof of the cathedral – a sound as superficial and profane as it might have seemed in a tomb. In the half-dark she walked into one of the silk ropes protecting a section of the floor and further down she stumbled over the raised edge of a commemorative plaque.

When she reached the end of the nave she stopped again. The cathedral was normally entered by two ordinary doors set at each side of the portico. On the morning of this day, however, the ornate bronze doors, panelled with reliefs of Old Testament scenes, had been opened for the hours of the ceremony and the small doors were barred from the inside and padlocked. She went to a side door that led out beside one of the chapels. but this had been locked with a key. With a moan of alarm, she twisted the handle, then turned back helplessly into the church. From the shadowed walls, the agonies, the depositions, the Pietàs looked down – but not at her. There is nothing to be done, they said – not addressing her.

There was a rustle in the transept, and quick footsteps. Someone had come in, through yet another door. There was now almost no light in the church and Sophie stood still by the wall while the unhesitating steps drew nearer – circumnavigating the silken rope, rising over the ridge of the plaque. The figure did not speak but came straight towards her. She herself could not utter a word. When they were face to face she saw that it was one of the domestics of the church – not a priest but a small elderly man in a black apron-like overall who sometimes admitted visitors to secluded chapels or, if they had obtained special permission, showed them into a room behind the altar to see the treasure of the church displayed behind glass.

He nodded to her politely, as if it were the most natural thing in the world to find her there that evening. He smelled like the church, of marble and incense and worn cloth. She began to explain, to apologize, her voice wavering, high-pitched, up the nave. He did not reply, but while she was talking drew a bunch of keys out of the square pocket of his overall. He sorted these expertly, without hurrying, and they dangled from his hand with a metallic rustle, being too large and too numerous to jingle. He fitted into the lock of the little door a key that might have opened the great gate of a city. The door swung back, letting in faint daylight and a rush of warm air.

Sophie thanked him. She stood in the doorway, looking into his grave face. He still had not spoken. It did not seem possible to tip him.

'Good evening,' she said.

'Good night.'

She ran down the few steps into the street. She heard the door being locked again behind her.

The square in front of the cathedral was empty. She crossed it and started at a half run down the road. She was now in a residential area, not prosperous but respectable. Lights had been turned on in the streets and in the rooms and the occasional shops that lined the sidewalk. (The way was so narrow that there was in fact no sidewalk, only a white painted strip to guide pedestrians; but tonight, in the absence of traffic, a thin stream of people had moved into the centre of the road.) Here the crowd was small and the faces cheerful. Only the children cried out in exhaustion, slung over their fathers' shoulders, clutching ribbons or tiny flags. There was no sign of the members of the procession. Rounding a bend in the road, Sophie slowed to an ordinary walk. A clock struck a quarter to eight. She had plenty of time.

She had plenty of time. As she walked along she smiled, from a sensation of deliverance, a disproportionate sense of danger past. It was night now. The lights were going on one after another, and from almost every doorway there were the smells of dinners being cooked, special dinners for the evening of a festival. The people in the street became fewer and fewer, then disappeared altogether. Looking up, she saw for the first time the shape of the gate ahead of her, its merlons and crenelations carved on the blue night sky and the stars. The road widened; she heard the swish of the cars on the highway outside. She began now to think of him and wondered if at this moment he might be there waiting for her beyond the gate, but she did not quicken her pace; there was something so delicious in this certainty of meeting that she went along more slowly still. As she left the sidewalk and crossed the open space to the gate, she changed the bag into her left hand and put up her right to arrange her hair. And in the shadow of the archway she hesitated – not in trepidation but from delight.

# Eight

Since they left Florence the dark had come down completely and the moon stood before them in the sky however the road turned. It was two days since the night of the festival and they were on their way home. They had been driving for several hours, and now she sat inclined towards him, her head lowered not quite to his shoulder. She touched him only with one hand, resting the tips of her fingers on a fold of his linen jacket.

The previous day, on their way to Florence, she had sat up straight beside him in the sun, her scarf tied over her hair, her elbow on the open window, his cigarettes and matches in her lap, and watched the woods and fields pass by. They played a game of identifying the trees, because he claimed she did not know their Italian names.

'*Questo, cos'è?*'

'*Lecio.*'

'*E quello?*'

'*Tiglio.*'

'*No – quercia.*'

Or they spoke about themselves, confirming to one another that they were there together.

'I was afraid you wouldn't be at the station.'

'I thought you wouldn't come.'

'So it seems that one must believe in miracles after all.

Not the miracles of the Church but of the railway station.'

'Just think – there must be miracles at the railway station every day.'

They had reached Florence in the afternoon, crossed the river, and found a place for the car near the cathedral. They went to lunch in a nearby restaurant, where, because of the lateness of the hour, they were almost alone – and where, because of their happiness, no one seemed to reproach them. When they came out of the restaurant, the city was reviving from the afternoon closing. They walked about the streets with their arms linked, he on the road and she on the narrow footpath. Almost everything they said was irrelevant.

'Ghiberti made the doors because Brunelleschi designed the dome.'

Or 'Look – they found the head of the Primavera.'

'Do you read Pratolini?'

'That's the Palazzo Strozzi.'

If they stopped to look at one another and to ask without speaking the same question over again and give the same reply, they walked on again smiling. They must have been smiling all day, she thought, from the pleasure of being together.

She discovered that he collected paintings of battles – an odd taste in someone so attached to life. In the Via de' Fossi they inquired in one antique shop after another without finding what he wanted.

'Do you have any battles?'

'No, signore, there are no battles here.' ... 'There aren't as many as there used to be.' ... 'No, we don't even expect any.'

He gave up the pursuit of battles and bought instead a pair of earrings – long, dusty gold loops that he fixed into her ears while she stood before the mirror in a cluttered shop.

It was cool in the early evening and they walked along the river. A group of young men were casting a net from a boat, one standing up to ship the oars against the current, the others spreading the lines of the net in the clouded green water. The boat swung very slowly in a half circle, resisting the river with an air of purpose and necessity that contrasted oddly with the evening bustle of the town. Lights from the bridge fell on the intent brown backs bent over the water and on the silent, upright figure of the oars-man.

'How strange.' The stone parapet of the Lungarno is exactly the right height for leaning, and she leaned on it. Inches from her back, the traffic roared past. 'This, in the centre of the city.' They looked at the boat and then into the river.

'D'Annunzio wrote a poem about the Arno.'

'Can you say it?'

'No.'

They leaned side by side, their bent elbows not meeting, their lowered faces not seeing.

'Oh, signorina.'

'Ah, Professor.'

The boat had drawn towards the opposite bank and they walked away, forgetting it.

'Do you remember where we left the car?'

Now she sat silent beside him on the dark road and he

could not be sure if she slept or not. When she moved her hand on his side, he glanced at her and saw that her eyes were open. 'Sleep, darling.'

'Yes. Yes.'

But she would not have slept for anything. Tilting her head she could see the red moon and the stars rising and lowering over the uneven road. The car rushed between rows of sloping pines whose trunks were barred with white paint, and past an army of advertisements for gasoline, Chianti, and men's hats. Once in a while they passed through a village whose main and single street shone like a fair with a confusion of neon lights, and in whose un-adorned cafés children, too late out of bed, slept on their mothers' laps. As clearly as if it were day she could pic-ture the symmetrical Tuscan landscape that extended on either side. She had made this journey from Florence a dozen times before without ever finding it too short, but tonight the numbered notices of decreasing kilometres seemed to be posted at every turn. She wanted to go on for ever – but wanted it intensely, as if it were a possibility – and wondered whether she had ever been as happy as this.

She put up her hand to his, on the wheel. 'There are no battles here.'

'And we don't even expect any.'

She withdrew her hand and replaced it at his side. 'I don't ever want to arrive.'

She would have a good dinner when they reached home, and a warm bath; she would wash her face and brush her hair, and they would make love. Even so, she did not want to arrive, for this safety, this perfection, would have passed, and there was no way to detain or even acknowledge it; no pact she could make, if she were willing, with that notoriously bad keeper of bargains, God.

He turned his head once more. 'Look at me. Will you love me as much as this tomorrow?'

He had asked this rhetorical question during the day and they had laughed at it. Now she turned her cheek against the hard leather and didn't reply. It was the question no one could answer, and her reason for not wanting to arrive. Whether tomorrow she would love him, or he her, as much as this, or more, or less, no one could say. The road, the city (whose lights and towers could now be seen below the stars), the warm bath, the comfortable bed and their sleep together, all brought that tomorrow closer. And the thread of her happiness was no stronger than the clasp of her fingers on his coat, no longer than this last mile of their journey.

# Nine

While they were sitting at lunch a great storm broke. At this time of year, the height of summer, there were brief thunderstorms almost every day, but this was something special. The sultry day was split by lightning – not crackling flashes but a series of full, silent illuminations, weird as moonlight – and by explosive thunder. Then the rain came down, white, torrential. The day darkened. The shutters of the dining room had to be closed, and they could hear one of the maids doing this throughout the house. Isabella, the old servant who was waiting on the table, switched on the lights, but a moment later the electricity failed, on a peal of thunder, and the three of them went on with their meal in the half-dark.

They were seated, Luisa and Sophie and Tancredi, at equal distances around the circular table, and were in this way quite far from one another. At first the storm was perfectly discussable. Luisa spoke about certain leaks in the upstairs rooms, cracks that she had meant to have repaired. Tancredi mentioned the risk to the threshing and the possible damage in the orchards. It was even a means of animating an awkward conversation, for this was the first time Luisa had seen Sophie since she had gone to live with Tancredi in his own house. They were in love, presumably. And why, Luisa had been wondering when the storm broke, did one qualify the situation to oneself in that way? One would always want to think of oneself as being on the side of love, ready to recognize it and wish it well – but, when confronted with it in others, one so often resented it, questioned its true nature, secretly dismissed the particular instance as folly or promiscuity. Was it merely jealousy, or a reluctance to admit so noble and enviable a sentiment in anyone but oneself? Charity, talent, love were real, perhaps, only to the sufferer and the beneficiary, and abstractions in the eyes of others.

When the storm began they were all glad of the interruption. There was quite a lively conversation about storms in general. Darkness, in this long, large room lined with furniture and dim paintings, drew them closer together. As it went on, however, the storm ceased to be welcome or even socially acceptable. The heavens gaped and roared above the house. Isabella ran out of the room with her hands to her ears and could be heard having hysterics in the kitchen. It was frightening in the way that an earthquake is frightening, because it was so immeasurably beyond anyone's control. Their talk subsided. They came to the end of the fruit and sat on around the table without speaking.

Or is it simply, Luisa went on to herself (turning up, as it were, the volume of her thoughts to make them coherent through the storm), that love so often makes for trouble, for such a fuss? Tancredi had a wife and children. And in Italy there is no divorce. It could only end badly for everyone concerned. (She included herself in this 'everyone'.) What a fuss about nothing. Then – No, she corrected herself; not about nothing. If it was a fuss, it was a fuss in the way that life itself is a fuss. She could concede them that.

'There *are* candles,' she said. But no one spoke.

She tried another conversation, about the crops, because the two of them began to seem quite chastened, as if she were censuring them as they sat there on either side of her. And in this way they passed the time, while the storm continued, until Sophie suddenly exclaimed: 'But this is awful!' Their minds were running so much in two directions that she herself added: 'This storm.'

'It's dying down,' Tancredi said. He moved his hand on the cloth as though he would reach over to comfort her, but the table was round and he and she across from each other. Indeed, the storm was receding. The lights came on again, but soon were not required. The hysterics in the kitchen ceased, and Isabella came back to remove their plates. They could hear the thunder going away, grumbling, in the direction of Rome.

'Let's see what's happened to the garden.' Luisa got up, pushing back her chair, placing her napkin on the table decisively, as if she were physically changing the trend of all their thoughts. She went through into the living room before the others had time to rise from their seats.

Tancredi came round the table to Sophie, but now it was he rather than she who seemed in need of comforting. He wanted to touch her in order to reassure himself, but Isabella was still clearing the table. He reached out and adjusted one of her ear-rings instead.

'Don't worry – it's not like that.' She said this as if she had understood Luisa's thoughts as well as his. They walked into the living room.

He said: 'It's not *like* anything.'

He helped Luisa to open the doors into the garden. It was still raining and from the trees and the eaves of the house large drops of water came splashing down like stones. The wind had died with the storm and the sky had cleared, but there was no sun, no colour whatever. The entire countryside looked blanched and beaten. On the surrounding hills, the crops, the vineyards, the harvested and freshly tilled fields might all have been of the same texture.

The garden had been treated with a violence that seemed almost intentional. A row of terra-cotta urns holding orange and lemon trees had been bowled off their pedestals and lay about the stone paths in the attitudes of the slain. Some of the urns had smashed, and rested in pools of their spilled red earth. Others had stayed intact, but in them the trees were crushed or broken. The fruit itself was cast about in the grass and the flower beds.

'What a sight it must have been,' Luisa said – unexpectedly, for the others were waiting for her to lament the losses – 'these great things reeling about, being swept off their perches.'

They came down the steps from the house. The whole length of the garden was littered with fallen flowers and with the dropped leaves of the trees. Taller plants were bent double and shorter ones laid against the earth. All the depressions of the grass and paths were filled with water. They walked slowly over squelching pebbles, around plots of petunias and dahlias. The rain ceased now altogether and a thin, chill breeze came up. There had been so many days of extreme heat that at first the sensation was practically unrecognizable. The palm trees swayed and water was shaken down from the oleanders and the laurel. Sophie folded her arms across her waist and shivered in her cotton dress.

'I'll get you my sweater from the car.' Tancredi went

around the house by one of the sodden paths and in a few minutes came back with an olive-green pullover. She arranged it across her shoulders with the sleeves hanging down on her breast.

Now the gardeners began to arrive and one or two labourers from a farm near the house. Luisa talked to them as they walked back and forth among the ruined urns, pointing out this and that – how one bush was virtually undamaged, another split in two. They paced about, like doctors and orderlies on a battlefield, assessing the situation before they went to work, taking account of the losses but more engaged with what could be saved. Tancredi went over to help the men lift up the urns. Four or five of them, pushing and struggling, finally forced a few unbroken vases back on to their stone blocks.

They all set to work – raking up the rubbish from the grass, staking and tying the larger plants and building up earth about the small ones. To Luisa this activity was instantly comforting. Why do we make such an issue of everything, she wondered, putting in order a row of zinnias, pressing the wet soil so firmly into place that her fingerprints remained around each plant. It was all in the course of events – things blowing about, being set to rights, flowering again. She thought: There is the resilience of things; these plants are designed with just such storms in mind. She said to herself: It is their nature.

Tancredi's labours had the opposite result. Ever since the dispiriting lunch, he had wanted to get away, to take Sophie home, to see how his own garden had fared. And now, with everyone manfully setting things to rights, it seemed impossible to leave. He watched Luisa rise from the plot of zinnias and survey the scene in her high-minded, high-handed way. He could not move. In the storm a fig tree had been wrenched away from a low wall that supported it, and he found himself holding it up in his arms while one of the gardeners attempted to truss its dangling branches. Water slid down the enormous leaves above his head and pelted his face and clothes. The man went to fetch a piece of cord, and Tancredi, still embracing the tree, leaned against the wall and looked across the garden at Sophie.

A boy was collecting the lemons in a hessian bag, and she was going about with him, picking up the fruit and handing it to the boy or dropping it in the bag. She had tied the sleeves of Tancredi's green pullover around her neck. Her hair was rather wet and hung flatly down against the sides of her head. Her dress was wet too and clung to the backs of her legs as she bent down to pick up the lemons. To Tancredi she looked unbearably mortal, a prey to her present circumstances, to himself, to mysterious events to come. She seemed so intent on her simple task, so fastidious – rubbing the muddied fruit on the grass before it went into the bag. Each time she looked up and handed another lemon to the boy, Tancredi felt a pang for her, as if she were giving away something precious of her own. He could not get over this impression of her vulnerability, though he reasoned with himself as he stood there propping up the dripping tree. He wished she would stop, go and sit on the steps, fix her hair, be more in command of herself; looking as she did at present, she was too great a responsibility for him.

As he watched her she did in fact come to the end of the lemons. She and the boy glanced about, found one or two more under the trees, and put them in the bag. Then she went, without offering to do anything more, and sat down on the highest of the few steps that led up to the house. She did not attend to her hair or her dress. At first she watched the activities in the garden. Then she looked up, as if she had been intending to do so all along, straight into Tancredi's eyes. He thought she would smile (for he knew that he looked ridiculous, standing there all wet grasping the wretched tree), but she looked for a moment more serious than ever, and when she did smile it was a smile in no way concerned with the tree.

She unfastened the sleeves of his pullover from about her neck. Then she held the pullover up so that she could pull it over her head. It was far too big for her, and in any case the breeze had died and the day was getting warm again. Nevertheless, sitting there on the steps, she put on his pullover. At that moment, in the presence of all these people, it was the closest she could come to taking him in her arms.

# Ten

They slept in a room upon whose high, high ceiling the painted branches were obligingly abundant with an equal variety of fruit and flowers. The white walls had at one time borne panels of a similar decoration, but these had to a large extent been worn away and even, around doors and windows, painted over. The blue-tiled floor had been trodden into slight undulations, the shutters were the colour of red earth, and the furnishings were few and massive. The bed was mounted on a low step between two windows. Its four corner posts, spirally carved, had been intended to support a canopy, which had long since disintegrated, leaving unobscured overhead the view of ripe oranges and full-blown roses.

'Is it getting late?'

'It's only seven. And the day will be as hot as ever, from the feel of it. . . . How can you be so cool? So cold and smooth. Like having a fish in one's bed.'

'Never had one. Besides, fish have scales.'

'Only if you rub them the wrong way.' He reversed the direction of his hand. 'What would you like to do today?'

'Let's think. Since it's Sunday, we might drive somewhere for lunch.'

'Or take a picnic with us.'

'We should try to stay off the main roads.'

'There's a place, a farmhouse, on the plain as you go towards the coast. There are some remains of a monastery – a wall and a fresco. I own land there, just a few acres. Perhaps you'd like that?'

'Then let's get up. We can have breakfast in the garden.'

They had breakfast in the garden almost every day. They sat together at a table under the trees and passed each other the bread and brushed the bees from the marmalade. It was now the end of August, and each morning produced a blazing sun, a desert sun that had strayed north from Africa. Beyond the house, farms and villages shimmered in the bleached countryside. There were no pedestrians on the roads, which the traffic covered at a feckless holiday speed. But in the garden there was always shade and sometimes a breeze.

Unlike Luisa's, this garden had not run wild; the hollyhocks, the dahlias, the marigolds were all as accomplished as the flowers on the painted ceiling. The pale climbing roses had been meticulously set in their patch of shade and the ferns fell over the stones as they had been trained to do.

Enclosed on two opposing sides by a low wall, the garden was a square large enough to include some splendid palms and a row of lime trees. The rosy colour of the wall could be seen only in the intervals of a hedge of thick clipped laurel. In the centre of the garden there was a well – a large circular stone well raised on a double pediment and arched over by a hoop of iron. The arms of the original owner of the house had been engraved on one side, and the other was looped with a garland of chipped stone roses. The well was no longer in use and had been closed with a grating. A circle of flowering plants stood on its broad rim, and above – from the centre of the iron hoop where a bucket should have been suspended – there hung a great pot of pink geraniums. At its far end, away from the house, the garden finished in a grove of ilexes. Out of sight beyond the trees, a sunken maze had been levelled to make a tennis court.

On its remaining side the garden was overlooked by the rear of the house. It was four storeys high and covered with uneven gold stucco, which seemed in the sun to be stretched like skin over the bricks, so that all the nerves and sinews of the house rippled beneath it. Staircases and fireplaces had been concentrated in this wing when the house was built, and there were no windows above the ground floor, except for a deep-set row of apertures belonging to servants' quarters under the roof. Long ago and almost at random, several false windows had been painted on the otherwise blank façade of the intervening storeys, and these were utterly charming. In one, the faded green make-believe shutters were completely closed; in another they were half open; on the sill of a third, a blue pot held a cluster of flaking marigolds. The house was high and finished in a moulded cornice supported by deep curving modillions.

'It's a pity to go anywhere, it's so lovely here.'

'We'll be back in the afternoon.'

'Is it far?'

'No, but a winding road. And we can't drive right up to the farm – there's nothing but a path for the last half mile. We'll have to leave the car on the road and walk across a field.'

The field, which for some time had not been ploughed or planted, was full of coarse grass and tough little shrubs that caught on Sophie's dress and scratched her bare legs. Tangled everywhere through this dry summer slope were thousands of red poppies. The path, a strip of trodden grass, led them over a slight incline and was quite unshaded. The only trees were the olives of surrounding fields and an occasional furled poplar. Renoir painted such a scene and called it 'The Upward Path' – even though the figures in his painting are descending.

Sophie and Tancredi had eaten their picnic in a wood of cypresses on one of the nearby hillsides, then driven down to the plain. Centuries before, this plain had been a shallow lake, and it was from this time that the monastery was dated. Even now the drained fields lay on the plain with a relapsed stillness of inland water, and the two figures waded through the grass as if through the shallows of a pool. It was afternoon and their slowly moving forms were the only sign of life as, one behind the other, they climbed the little rise.

Tancredi, in cotton trousers and a blue shirt, brushed his way along the rough field, sometimes humming and sometimes absent-mindedly singing a song. From time to time he put his hand back to help Sophie over a small ditch or an outcropping of stone – as though, like Orpheus, he were in some way prevented from turning to her. The day was so hot that even this brief contact made the sweat start in their hands. The sun dazzled them and burned their necks and their bare heads.

He broke off singing. He glanced over his shoulder. 'You must be dying.'

'Not yet.'

'It isn't as far as it looks. We'll be there in a few minutes.'

'Will they mind my coming?'

'They'll be delighted.'

'How many are there?'

'In the family? Oh – an old couple, who must be practically incapacitated; then Filomena, who is my age and used to be beautiful. Her husband died in the war. Nelda, her daughter, who was married last year to Nestore from the village up there. Now he lives here and works the farm, because Nelda's brother is learning to be a mason. . . . Well, there it is.'

They had reached the top of the rise. Before them was a clump of poplars through which a web of vines had been pleached into a thick curtain. To the left of these trees there was a low stone farmhouse, yellow grey with a red roof and one tall brick chimney. At right angles to it, there stood another building of the same size. Shrubs and flowering creepers had been grown against all the walls, perhaps as protection from the sun on days like this. There were no ruins to be seen. There was no garden; the cultivated fields came right up to the house, but where they rose into a bank before the front wall the poppies were growing in such profusion that the sea of crops appeared to have broken there in a great wave of red.

As they approached the house Tancredi stopped, beside the group of trees. Sophie drew level with him, and they stood for a moment looking at each other in this shade that was no more than a dappling of the heat. It was too warm to embrace. He put his hand to her hair and they smiled at one another.

How happy we are, she thought, without the slightest

reflection or attempt to establish cause – as someone might marvel at a wonder of nature.

'How happy you look.' He kissed her forehead lightly and they went on. There was room now for them to walk side by side, and the path led through cultivated land. There was no one in sight – not even an animal or a chicken to be seen. All the shutters of the house were closed.

'Perhaps we should have let them know we were coming,' she said.

He looked at her in surprise. 'They'll be delighted,' he said again.

A woman in a black dress and black stockings came out of a side door, saw them, and called loudly – not to them but into the room behind her. She disappeared, and they heard other voices. The house visibly stirred, although the shutters remained closed. As they reached the front door, which was set above two steps, the same woman came out, smiling and followed by a girl in a black blouse and skirt. 'Signorino,' the woman said, and shook hands with Tancredi and laughed with pleasure. She was not tall, but dark and stately, with a refined, cheerful face and a smooth broad brow.

The girl then put out her hand, though more tentatively. She stood aside, smiling, to let them come in. Sophie thought, going first into the dark house: They *are* delighted.

'Filomena,' Tancredi said in an authoritative voice. 'Can we have some light?'

Filomena went to unlatch the shutters, and the girl, Nelda, pulled chairs out from a centre table. Tancredi and Sophie sat down, hardly able to see one another. The room smelled strongly of all its history – of meals, of children, of sleep and hard work.

A hot half-light was let in by Filomena, and at once, in a corner of the room, a baby began to cry. It was Nelda's new baby, a little boy, and she went and picked him up and brought him to the table, where, still yelling, he was handed about to be admired.

'Where's Nestore?'

'In the other room,' Filomena answered. The house was apparently divided into only two rooms. 'He went to get the old people out of bed.'

There appeared to be no question of protesting this. The old people must be awakened; not only would they *want* to get out of bed, they would be delighted.

Nelda rocked the baby and smiled shyly down at its head. Tancredi leaned both his elbows on the table and clasped his hands before him; this gave him the air of conducting an interview as he questioned Filomena about the farm. The questions were not idle, and these were evidently matters he wished to know about.

Sophie had never seen him in quite this role before. His authority, their humility, made her uneasy. No one seemed to mind but her. She looked around the room.

It was not a large room, and it had been asked to accommodate a great deal. There was the round wooden table, grooved and glossy with age, at which they sat, and this was surrounded by six unvarnished chairs with woven rush seats. A small marble-topped table stood in one corner; on it was set a white enamel stove with two burners, and beside it a dark green cylinder of gas. Apart from an urn on the stone floor, there was no sign of water – which might have been drawn from a well. One end of the room was entirely taken up with a vast, sagging wooden bed draped with a red coverlet, and next to this stood the baby's cradle. Above in the beamed roof was the only truly new and truly sordid object in the room – a naked circle of fluorescent lighting, for the moment inactive. A faint glow came from a miniature shrine fixed in the wall above the stove – a tiny bulb, trailing a too heavy cord, lit a plastic image of the Madonna wreathed in faded paper flowers and backed by a card with a printed text.

Nestore appeared, a short and wiry young man with a brown face worn not by anxiety but by hard work and the weather. Tancredi got up, and there was some bustle about bringing in the old people. The old man still showed signs of having been dressed for church that morning; he wore a collarless blue shirt and thick grey trousers that came stiffly to his armpits and were supported by canvas braces. A few strands of grey hair had been combed back across his head. His eyes were a very pale blue and out of them he gave a bewildered look of recognition to Tancredi.

The old woman was more alert. She bowed her birdlike little head practically to Tancredi's fingers. Her face still had some colour not due to the sun, and her manner showed that she had once been pretty.

They all sat on the hard chairs. There was a short respectful silence, as though grace were being said, and then Nestore began to talk about the land. Now everyone had their hands clasped before them on the table. Tancredi's – confident, capable, well kept; the hands of the old couple were of the texture and colour of a walnut; Nestore's, almost as broad as they were long; Filomena's and Nelda's, reddened and not really in repose, stealing an unaccustomed holiday. And Sophie's own hands – shapely and soft, the nails carefully painted, one white wrist turned upward and circled by a gold bracelet.

Nestore's hand was lifted from the table and extended towards Tancredi in a gesture that was apologetic without being sorry. 'We had to support the others,' he was saying.

Tancredi shrugged. 'Perhaps they thought they were supporting you.' He turned his head to Sophie. 'The threshing,' he said. 'There was a strike over the threshing. The farm labourers wanted higher wages.'

'Did they get them?' she asked, hoping so.

'Not what they wanted,' he replied, and then he smiled at Nestore and again shrugged his shoulders. The whole family seemed to shrug in response, but there was a silence, an awkwardness. The old couple were almost asleep.

Filomena pushed back her chair. 'Will you have a glass of wine?'

'I think not,' Tancredi said, 'since we have to climb up to the fresco.' Everyone smiled again and he turned back to Sophie. 'We have to go up a ladder. The fresco is on the upper part of a wall.' He unclasped his hands and spread them out flat on the table. 'Shall we go?'

Nelda woke her grandmother and gave her the baby. The old woman supported the child on her knee with one practised arm and looked at it with pleased detachment.

They left the house by a back door and crossed a hot little yard to the other building that Sophie had seen from the field.

Nelda, walking behind with Sophie, said timidly: 'Your dress is pretty.' She touched her own black skirt. 'This is so hot, this black.'

Sophie asked cautiously: 'Could you wear a lighter colour?'

'Ah,' said the girl, with another suggestion of a shrug. 'It's mourning for my husband's mother. We wear black for a year. For that,' she said, with the air of citing an unalterable law, 'is the custom in this country.' She meant the word 'country' to apply merely to what could be seen around them.

The other stone building was a combination of two structures of differing heights. The first, which they did not enter, was apparently used as a cowshed and barn, and stood open to the yard with a pair of immense wooden doors propped back by stones. The second building had similar doors and they were closed.

Nestore struggled with the bolts of these doors, and Tancredi came over to Sophie. 'Are you getting tired?'

'Oh no.' But she was standing with her head lowered and one hand up to shield her eyes from the glare.

'Does all this depress you?'

She shook her head, and gave a shrug like Nelda's.

'As soon as we've seen the fresco we'll go home.'

She found it incredible that they should be able to extricate themselves within a few minutes from the world she saw here. Tancredi's villa and their life in it appeared to her, for the moment, inordinately pleasurable, and Tancredi himself the beneficiary of privilege so all-pervasive that it could not even be described as entrenched. She wanted to apologize for the disproportion, confronted with this other existence. She half turned away, but at this moment the doors swung back and Nestore called to them to enter the building.

The interior was well lit, through a series of long slits

near the roof. The floor was of stone, irregularly flagged and bare except for a few implements. The shed might have been reserved for winter storage but at present showed no sign of use. At the far end a high wall provided the division from the adjoining building. The character of this wall was in no way related to any of the surroundings in which it found itself. It stood apart, as it might have stood in an open field. It was like a strip torn from a magnificent illumination. The fresco covered the wall almost completely. The background was a dark, burnt red and had been much damaged by the damp – it was mottled with little craters of mould. The lower half of the fresco was discernible only in vague shapes and a broken pattern of formal decoration. Higher up, higher than eye level, there was a seated central figure rather larger than life-size, surrounded by saints and angels and balancing a child on one knee in the same matter-of-fact way that Nelda's grandmother had held the baby. This child was less an infant than a diminutive man. The Madonna, whose inclined face was a pale, almost featureless oval, was draped in a blue robe that also covered her head. Out of the robe and on to her shoulders streamed tendrils of corn-coloured hair. Her knees, beneath the fluted folds of blue, were set apart.

There had been no attempt at restoration. The fresco was in an advanced state of decay. The impression it made was unaccountable; there was nothing in any of its details to suggest the splendour of the whole.

There were no signs of other ruins. Nothing remained of the other rooms of the monastery, which had been abandoned, perhaps, and then demolished when the farm was built.

'No one knows who is responsible,' Tancredi was saying. It was not clear whether he referred to the destruction or to the fresco.

Nestore brought the ladder, and this was fixed, with some unheeded scraping, against the upper part of the fresco. Tancredi climbed up and pointed out to Sophie from above the details that could still be seen – the disintegrating stars on the robes of the saints, the powdery remains of gilt circlets about the heads of angels. Enraptured, they all smiled. 'Isn't it beautiful?' they asked her. 'Isn't it beautiful?'

Tancredi had seen it often, and he came quickly down and held the ladder for her.

The steps of the ladder were round and springy. She felt herself to be exceedingly brave, since she climbed up in the full expectation of falling. The higher she went the more the ladder wobbled – she couldn't imagine how it had stayed so securely in place for Tancredi. She did not go all the way up, but stopped near the top, her face level with the blank countenance of the Virgin. There she stayed for some moments, eye to nonexistent eye, gripping the edges of the ladder. The pallid, erased face, only slightly larger than her own, had less the look of decay than of some utter forgetfulness, some monumental knowledge never imparted and now irretrievably mislaid.

She started to climb down.

'The stars,' called Tancredi. 'Did you see the stars?'

'Yes,' she said. And then: 'I think so.'

They all laughed. *Brava!* they cried out as she put her foot down on the stone floor, and she herself laughed with relief and pleasure. She felt safe to look up at the fresco once more. But, having come so close, it had now receded farther from her than before – seemed hopelessly effaced. Yet her earlier impression stayed, and was the clearer one.

'Now we should be getting home,' Tancredi said. They walked out into the sun.

They shook hands, all of them, with great formality as though after the presentation of a medal.

'Don't stand here in the heat.'

'Can you find the way?'

'Many thanks.'

'Not at all.'

They didn't speak to one another walking across the first field, passing the cluster of trees. He saw that she was happy again, so there was no question to ask. When they reached the rise they looked back and waved. Filomena, Nestore, and Nelda stood in the doorway of the house, and now Nelda held the baby in her arms. But when they passed the crest of the hill, they were once more alone in the world. He took her hand as before because the rough grass, folding under their feet, was slippery as they went down. At one point he stopped and turned back to kiss her, and then they went on. As he did this he did not even look about – for this afternoon it was completely deserted, this country. There were just the solitary trees, the lake of grasses and red flowers, and two figures descending the upward path.

# Eleven

Tancredi said: 'My father – whom you knew –'

'Of course,' said Luisa, from the bed.

'– liked to think of himself as detached. As being scarcely influenced by material considerations or by circumstances. The first being largely within his control and the second completely beyond it, he could afford to adopt such an attitude. Actually he was unable to contend with any sort of reality, and this was his means of protecting himself.'

'Sensible,' Luisa suggested. She moved her head to a cool place on the pillow but kept her eyes on Tancredi.

He shrugged. 'He was a man of certain capacities, yet he never put these to any use, not even for his own satisfaction, because he feared the judgement of the world – feared, in fact, the unforeseeable consequences of any kind of action. He philosophized out of his own weakness. Afraid to compete with others, he chose to achieve nothing and to exonerate himself by referring to all men as equals.'

'He may have believed it,' she said.

'He did not. His attitude, rather, was that he had magnanimously spared them his competition. Never having ventured, he implied he would have won.'

'You're hard.'

'He invented his own life and the lives of those who impinged on him. After my mother's death he created for her a character she had never possessed, and in this way managed to efface her memory for all of us. It was impossible for us, as children, to refer to our mother as having been in any degree fallible, or even human. We wouldn't have required my father to mention her faults – which were relatively few. Had he merely implied that she occasionally cut her fingernails or brushed her teeth like the rest of us, I believe we would have embraced him. After a while the memory of my mother became boring – it was that boredom that attaches to any matter of which the truth may never be told. The very idea of her, circumscribed as it was at my father's insistence, was a renunciation of one's intelligence. He never remarried, and never had another association with a woman, as far as anyone knew. It was surprising he had married in the first place – one could scarcely credit him with so much organization. His life, as I've said, was a total unreality. He cut himself off from truth, from all tangible things.'

Luisa said: 'Sometimes, surely, truth is closer to imagination – or to intelligence, to love – than to fact? To be accurate is not to be right.'

'Oh – sometimes, sometimes,' he said impatiently. She would not let him rest with his point of view. This caused him a physical uneasiness, and he shifted about, crossed one knee over the other. If she had not been ill, he would have lit a cigarette. She had been in bed for a week, though he had only heard of her illness that morning. It was odd, he thought, how the idlest gossip went round the district

95

at once, while an important fact was never repeated. 'But equally, don't you agree, one can't live without *some* facts; without anything – *attestable*.'

So this is why you make so many commitments, thought Luisa. 'So this is why,' she remarked, 'you became an architect.'

He smiled. He lounged back in the chair. That was more like it, more what he had come for – to be explained and understood and put at his ease. The day was close, and this shuttered room smelling a little of medicines – or so he imagined, perhaps, because he saw the bottles there beside the bed – was a refuge, a hermit's cave. He always considered her a sage – someone who could give the meanings of the riddles, show him how to make the puzzles come out. But that made her sound more like a conjurer at a fair. He didn't come to see her perform, it wasn't that – he came only when he really needed her. (This did not give the right impression either, because his feeling for her was sincere.) She was never disappointing – as others ultimately were, betraying at last by a word or a gesture that they were just as proud, as revengeful, as ambitious as anyone else.

He couldn't understand why he had suddenly felt impelled to say these things about his father. It was all true enough, but it was something he seldom thought of now. He had had, like everyone else, an exceptionally unhappy childhood, but his later memories, of adolescence, were predominantly pleasant ones. These memories were frequently represented in single scenes, like paintings – paintings in clear colours, well preserved, perhaps a little over-cleaned. Sometimes he would see himself, a tall young man, walking on the unpaved country roads in the morning. (In these memories he was always taller, it was always morning, and the roads were still unspoiled by asphalt.) At other times he was on the beach at Pesaro, at his family's summer house – studying while the others bathed, because he was usually sitting examinations in those days. Or with his sister – he in a white suit, she in a straight yellow dress that reached to her calf. This memory was particularly piercing, for Gabriella had been a tall, pliant beauty, a tulip of a girl, romantically sheltered, with no presentiment of the nervous spinsterhood in store for her. Looking at Luisa, Tancredi wondered: How can you bear it, this memory, this recollecting of things utterly and unthinkably past? He himself was already finding it intolerable to remember – not merely the people he would never speak with again, or the houses in which he could never hope to see them, but fragments of mood, light, sensation, which he couldn't recapture and which, revealing themselves to him only in the subsequent act of remembering, then seemed to remain permanently and to accumulate significance in direct proportion to their increasing remoteness in his experience. The very word experience, at that moment, was more poignant to him than grief or love.

Then how shall I bear this later on, he wondered – for all the while he had in some way been thinking of Sophie and marvelling at the sadness he was storing up for himself. How shall I stand it?

'Your memory is a little harsh,' Luisa said.

He stared at her.

'We were talking of your father.'

'Ah yes.'

'He was a scholar. He had taken the trouble to

know many things – to know them thoroughly, that is.'

Tancredi nodded. 'He seldom erred, and never on the side of generosity.'

Luisa gave him up, her hand briefly lifted from the sheet to brush away his last remark. They were silent.

'I'm afraid you're tired,' Tancredi said at last. He stood up, a darker, heavier, shorter man than the figure of his reminiscences. And older. He said: 'She will be waiting for me.'

'I've been thinking that.'

'I came straight from town. She doesn't know yet that you're ill.' Tancredi found the greatest difficulty in speaking of Sophie to Luisa. He could not bring himself to utter her name. He said, speaking as though he were dictating a formal letter of sympathy: 'I hope you're going to be well soon. I was so sorry to learn you were ill.'

'Nothing serious,' she said, taking his hand and smiling. 'It gives me a chance to be alone with my thoughts.'

It's all very well for you, he thought peevishly, with *your* thoughts.

'Give her my love.'

'Of course she'll come to see you.'

'I would like that.'

He kissed her hand and laid it back on the sheet, but he went on standing there looking at her. She was so composed, so prepared for anything, that he suddenly thought: Are you going to be really ill? Are you going to die? 'Are you going to be all right,' he asked, 'if I leave you now?'

'They'll come as soon as you've gone. And there's the bell – I only have to ring.'

He went to the door. 'And forgive me,' he said, 'for taking up so much time with talk about my father – whom in any case, you knew as well as I.'

'Whom I knew,' she said.

# Twelve

'It's nothing serious.' He put down his glass and went on with his meal. 'Or so she says.'

'I must go to see her,' Sophie said.

'I spoke with the family before I left. Her son is there – the banker, what's his name, Giorgio. They didn't seem alarmed.'

'I'll go on Friday,' she said.

'Or tomorrow,' he suggested.

'But tomorrow – we were going to drive to the mountains.'

He thought: She has a streak of ruthlessness. He looked at her to chart this new discovery, but found after all only the desire to be with him. When people say 'a streak' like that, he reflected – 'So-and-So has a streak of something' – it is always in a pejorative sense: a streak of cruelty, of cowardice, of dishonesty. Kindness, sympathy, affection were considered more pervasive, apparently did not come in streaks.

'Otherwise,' he went on, 'she was as always. Very calm, imposing.'

'She has a noble streak.'

After a moment Tancredi said: 'She said something strange – something that never occurred to me.'

'What?'

'A remark she made about my father. Not even a remark – merely a tone of voice, as I was leaving.' He hesitated again. 'No, nothing.'

For another idea had come to him now, and he stopped eating and looked again at Sophie. Everything he had said to Luisa that morning about his father had been directed at Sophie; it was only a step from his father's unrealities to hers. The total lack of reference, in her behaviour with him, to her present position caused him, he realized, precisely the claustrophobic sensations he had been describing an hour earlier. It was as if she had taken leave of her senses – or come into their full possession at the expense of her reason; as if she had no capacity to consider her actions in the light of their consequences, as if she thought it could go on for ever, this disregard for the eventual course of her life, and his. She surely could not imagine that he had always lived this way, in such seclusion, with no expression of his personality other than as a lover. If only she had once asked him: 'What are we to do?' or 'What is to become of us?' – that, he felt distractedly, was all he asked. It seemed little enough – the least indication that she made in her mind some connexion with external things. What of the continuity of her own existence? She lived within society, a society that required one to give an account of oneself – not even a good account, but an account. He felt quite indignant on behalf of her relatives and friends, who must expect her home or look for news of her. The earth might be uninhabited, from the way she behaved.

Today, arriving at the house, Tancredi had found the certainty of her presence almost frightening. On weekdays, before lunch, Sophie went to sit at the end of the garden in the shade of the trees, and she waited there for him to come home. She could not hear the car, which arrived on the other side of the house, but she felt his presence before she heard his step and, not looking up from her book or letter, would smile with pleasure. He was sometimes late, but she stayed on in the garden until he came, although the sun began to burn through the trees and the cook's son, who waited at table, looked out of the house repeatedly in despair.

Today, for the first time, he had almost expected, almost wished for, some disappointment – to find her, perhaps, more meagre, more pallid, diminished in his eyes like a cherished place revisited after an absence. Instead, of course, she had been disturbingly beautiful, dishearteningly pleased to see him. Glancing into her smiling, upturned face as he leaned down to kiss her, he had found it incredible that this woman had ever looked at him in any other way. She had once told him – and he longed to remind her of it – that their association was a threat to her; at one time, he knew, she had considered him unreliable and vain. He could scarcely believe that she had ever said such a thing, ever had a critical opinion of him. That time when she had coolly judged him now presented itself to him as a time of happiness.

Her love is perfect, he thought. What one always hears about – perfect love. Then he told himself, with relief and a certain satisfaction: I am not worthy of that. Not up to it at all. I am an ordinary person – a fallible, inconsistent, mortal man. Each adjective was successively pleasant to him, and he said them over in his head.

'Shall we walk a little?' he asked her, putting his

napkin by his plate and pushing away the unfinished meal. 'Is it too warm for you?'

She got up and walked to the edge of the covered terrace where they had been sitting. He came and took her arm, and they went down the double step and into the garden.

'What a lovely dress,' he suddenly said to her. Her beauty had seemed to him so remarkable as they sat at table that he could not keep from making at least this indirect reference to it. She was wearing a simple dress of a splendid colour, the sort of dress that might turn up in one of his memories.

She did not reply, and when they had reached the end of the path he said to her, knowing that he was actually speaking of his own preoccupation: 'What's the matter?'

She sat on the low stone wall that ran along the end of the garden. 'You're strange today.'

'Am I?' he said in corroboration.

She was running her hand slowly over the stone, stirring dust and bringing alarmed ants out of crevices. She was not looking at him, nor yet away. 'Why is that?'

'Why do you think it is?' he asked idly, trying to collect himself because he knew that he must speak to her and that the matter was very serious.

'Oh – you might be tired. You might be angry. It might be anything.' She brushed her palms together, dusting them off, and went on in the same way: 'You might have stopped loving me.'

'Why would I do that?' he asked with an inflection of real interest, as if he would be genuinely grateful to know.

'Oh,' she said again, 'I don't know. There wouldn't need

to be an explanation – not a plausible one, that is.' Having cleaned her hand, she put it back on the dusty wall. 'Anything might happen. You might find that you didn't like the colour of my eyes.'

He said gravely: 'I don't think that could ever be the reason.' He put out his hand and turned her face up to his. He said again: 'No. It could never be that.' And again he spoke with a note of literal meaning, as though he were turning over the suggestion in his mind.

He dropped his hand, and she lowered her eyes. It seemed to him that he was more engaged than ever in this newly discovered dream world of hers; in the same way it had become more necessary for him to speak. He felt like a man obliged to commit some demeaning act, some sickening petty theft that, while leaving its victim destitute, will not bring any material benefit to himself. He must break into this state of hers not in order to make himself happy but only so that his existence might be comprehensible to him. He had not faced the possibility of losing her. He loved her still. It was the unreality of her attitude that was intolerable to him.

He thought, with an almost comic sense of his own situation: How absurd it is to propose to us that our actions are altogether composed of influences and the effects of our circumstances; that we are irrevocably cut off from our own will. There comes a moment when one must utter a single sentence, and the immense effort involved in that utterance is unmistakably the expenditure of will. He looked at her closely, still hoping to detect some justifying fault. But as before, when he had examined her face for a trace of callousness, she defeated him, and he could only see her as she was to appear in his memory. It was, so to speak, the reverse of saying to oneself: 'I shall remember this'; he felt rather that here was a recollection, which must first be lived through. Since his nostalgia for her was inevitable, he preferred to embark on it as soon as possible – even in her presence.

He was about to speak; or so he told himself, as he sat there silent. Exchanging in his mind one pretext for delay after the other, he was like someone who, at the close of a beautiful day, constantly shifts his chair to enjoy the last of the light.

She said: 'Don't be anxious to find a reason.'

He had forgotten what they were saying. She saw that, and added: 'To come to the end of this.'

He smiled at her vaguely, as if it were all a joke.

In the same patient voice, she continued: 'Since there's no need. Since we don't have much time left together.'

The astonishment Tancredi felt at being thus relieved in an instant of any necessity to describe their position had nothing to do with a sense of deliverance – for by demolishing his belief in her unawareness of their dilemma she automatically brought into focus the dilemma itself, and he was faced not with discussion of the thing but with the thing itself. He felt a perverse disappointment that his concept of her love as an ideal love, something intact and indifferent to everything but its object, had turned out to be fictitious and that she was after all touched by the same earthly questions as himself. But what was strangest of all to him, and most interesting, was the revelation that she had in reserve these thoughts, perhaps limitless thoughts, of which he could have no knowledge; that her ideas might be entirely at variance with his assessment of them just when he was convinced he understood them best. This fascinated him – in the same way that the realization that his father and Luisa had been lovers had fascinated him by introducing into his father's life some of those very facts whose absence he had deplored and, along with them, the possibility of others equally well concealed.

He put up his hand again and turned her face towards him. Mysteriously, she had managed to keep some part of her mind aloof, and for the first time he sincerely wondered what she thought of him – that is, as distinct from what she loved in him. At the very moment when he had thought her most committed to him, she had shown herself to be to some extent detached, and her self-possession struck on him bleakly in spite of his relief. He had a presentiment of her restraint, of a capacity to deal, unbearably, with those matters that he himself could only deplore.

The prospect of losing her would not, after all, arrange itself conveniently into the landscape of his experience; it remained a prospect, an unknown and terrible loss in store, and refused to be grappled with in advance. By acquiring substance, as today he had wished her to do, she had become more singular and more dear to him, and their attachment to one another appeared to be much more complicated than he had imagined when he was dealing merely with realities.

# Thirteen

'Strange that no one comes.'

They had arrived at the house some minutes ago but were still sitting in the car. From the way he spoke they might have been completely dependent on the intervention of others to separate them.

'They can't have heard. I'll go in now.' Yet she made no move to leave him. Every parting had become suggestive, a rehearsal, and neither wanted to initiate it. Circumstances would intervene; there was no reason to precipitate them.

'I'll come for you at one,' he said. 'All right? Down here at one.' Soon she is going away, he thought, where I can't come to fetch her. I will never see her again. *Probably* never see her again, he emended, retreating. Then, since it was impossible for him to think that way, he fell back on the unpredictability of events, the strange accidents of life. Something might change, something would happen. So often when one planned for happiness, chance came between, spoiled everything. Why, in that case, should one count on the reverse? The worst need not happen either. Ah, but the worst *could* happen – and had happened to him several times in his life, all the more terrible for having been foreseen and having followed its foreseeable course. In despair from this clumsy sparring with his reason, he turned to her and lifted her hand on to his knee. Soon she is going away and I will never see her again. He was to bear a double weight of loneliness, his own and hers. It seemed to him that they were doing an obscure, outmoded thing in parting from each other. At one time partings were a recognized and tragic part of life. History and literature and song were full of enforced separations, dramatic farewells. But nowadays – was it because one travelled more easily, or because one acted with less finality? – people did not part. On the contrary, contemporary tragedy seemed to be bound up with their staying together. If they ceased to be lovers, they saw one another still; even divorced couples met on friendly terms (though he had always thought this a particularly unnatural way of doing things). It was unheard-of now to say good-bye for ever. In all the world, so it seemed to Tancredi, only he and she were compelled to part. It made them seem more cut off than ever from ordinary life. It gave their love a mismanaged and dated aspect, a terrible privacy.

It had been a week of days that were strange in their light and atmosphere, each one distinguished from ordinary time like the unreal, unclouded day of a celebration or the eve of an important journey. So much did this seem to Tancredi a part of his own condition that he was surprised to find the whole countryside speaking of it as an exceptional autumn – for the changing season had made, to him, no more than a monumental setting for Sophie's departure. There had been no mellowness and little decay. The weather was still and dry, and the leaves, when they did fall, lay for a long time in brittle circular patterns around the trees, like fragments of broken glass. This strange premonitory element seemed to be literally a trick of the light, since each evening brought a short, consoling respite.

He never thought at all of the time when she would be gone, never wondered what he would do with himself – if he might go away for a while, whether he would be reconciled with his wife. And when he remembered the time before he and Sophie met, he never felt that this could have been avoided. If someone had reminded him that he could have kept away from her, that this need not have developed, it would have been meaningless to him – as if an immunization had been discovered for a mortal disease he had already contracted.

She took her hand off his knee and opened the door with an abrupt gesture, then stayed a moment longer. 'I haven't brought anything.' Almost comically, like a suspect, she showed him her empty hands.

'It doesn't matter, she has everything she needs. It's you she wants to see.'

'Down here at one then.' She slid out of the car. She went up the steps, and was ringing the doorbell as he drove away.

It was no longer necessary to keep the shutters closed against the heat, and now the interior of the house was light in the mornings. There were flowers in the tiled hallway and on the landing of the stairs – florists' flowers, intended for the sickroom.

'How is she, Isabella?' Sophie asked the old woman who showed her up the staircase and down a corridor – for Luisa's room was at the back of the house.

'Less bad,' said Isabella, making it plain by a grimace that she was quoting the doctor. 'Less bad – what kind of a consolation is that? They've sent for a specialist. Poor thing, she's so weak. This morning she cried.'

They had reached the door, and Sophie hesitated a moment longer with her hand raised to knock. Luisa's tears were astonishing, even indecent.

This was one of the smaller bedrooms, which Luisa had preferred for its view – of a sky, a hillside, a grooved orchard, and a farmhouse of rusty tiles and rough stone. The room was sturdily furnished with things that were old-fashioned rather than old. There was a chest of drawers, a small blue velvet Victorian sofa, a bookcase, flowers on a table, and a low bed. In the mornings the room was filled with sunlight.

For many days now Luisa had scarcely left this room. Sitting up in bed supported by pillows, she received a few visitors, wrote a few letters, read, or looked out at the view. When the books that were brought to her became too heavy to hold, she sometimes lay for hours, scarcely thinking, though she was in complete command of herself. Her life seemed very long to her. Strangely, it had kept, in retrospect, a certain course and had even acquired a certain form – so much of a form that it was like a finished thing, she thought, awaiting only some dexterous stroke of termination. She would not have claimed that she now desired death – that was not in her character, and in any case she would have thought it an affectation, an imposition, to say so. Love of life was still strong in her; that morning she had wept, on waking, to find herself no better. Yet she did not quite believe she would recover, could not quite imagine herself deeply engaged again in her own concerns and those of others. When she learned that Sophie was coming, she thought about this love affair as one might think of a life in another age or on another planet – with curiosity and good-will but with immense remoteness and even with a sense of safety.

Her life, her long life, so she was thinking at this moment, had reached some point – not of completeness, perhaps, but of sufficiency. Although she had often been grieved by her own actions and those of others, she could hardly think of anything she wished undone. This was not from any sense of the perfection of the whole but from a now manifest continuity – and possibly because the imperfections had been so numerous that it would not be possible to subtract them and have anything left to assess. If she had sometimes been made aware that she was less rancorous and less infirm than many others, or more passionately anxious to understand, she attributed this to propitious circumstances, to the favourable conditions of her youth, the good influences of her friends and family. It was this benevolently directed course of her life that she now felt she could discern. What deflection could she herself have made that would have materially altered it? It amused her to think that she might have been lying in bed in a different room, staring through a window at quite another scene – for she did not doubt that she would have fallen ill just the same. She was smiling when Sophie came in.

It was not until Sophie bent over her and kissed her that Luisa collected herself. She pressed her visitor's hand and greeted her, and added: 'Forgive me – I was wandering in my mind, though only in a literal sense. On days like this, at the beginning of autumn, one has an idea of how it must be to live in those mountain villages where the air is always clear. I was wondering whether I would be the same, you know, if I had led a different life in another place.' She turned on her side, pushing back the sheet, for it was warm with the sun in the room. 'Everything here is beautiful.' She indicated the window. 'All conducive to the right choice, or to no choice at all. Perhaps if we lived with less physical beauty we would develop our true natures more.'

Sophie sat in a chair beside the bed. 'I feel it's too late now,' she said – as if she and not Luisa might be going to die – 'to be different.' She was thinking of Tancredi. Probably Luisa would speak to her of Tancredi. Seeing Luisa ill like this – much more ill than she had supposed her to be – Sophie was amazed at her own self-engrossment; she was like a guest who insists on having special food no matter what the inconvenience to others.

Luisa said: 'I should like to talk to you about Tancredi.' She was silent for a moment, and smiled. 'Having taken Tancredi as a subject for discussion, how hard it is to begin. He was here, of course, the other day.'

'How did you think he looked?' Sophie asked this conventional question seriously, for information. She had lost the sense of Tancredi's appearance. She could no longer imagine his face at all when he was not with her – as we are sometimes unable to conjure up our own image without looking in a mirror, so much is it part of our entire existence. She could not recall whether his eyes were brown or green, his nose straight or bent, whether he wore glasses all the time or just for reading. She would promise herself to notice these things when they were together. But she forgot or, if she remembered, the details did not help her to picture him when he was next away. And now that they were to be parted she wondered whether her first clear impression would come back to her much later, months from now, when they were no longer bound to one another.

'I thought,' Luisa replied slowly, 'he was more serious than I had ever seen him. It was curious to see him like that.' One is apprehensive about the wrong things, she thought; in the beginning I was afraid for her, because of what his life had been. Instead, she has preserved her ability to act in a way that will be unthinkable to him. 'You –' She reached out to touch Sophie. 'You are used to being serious, but he is not.' She spoke almost warningly, as though one more bout of seriousness might kill him.

Sophie said: 'It won't be for much longer. I'm going away.' In saying this, her mouth lost its proper control, so that the words came out distorted, giving her a new, untraceable accent.

Luisa said nothing. She wrapped her thin bed jacket more closely over her breast – protecting herself from such persistence, such pain; guarding, so to speak, the safety she had felt that morning.

Sophie went on, in this foreigner's voice that had mastered the grammar but not the shape of the words: 'I'm going away. There's nothing else to do.' Her words, which expressed the lack of an alternative, might also have referred to the completion of an experience.

Luisa now said thoughtfully, truthfully: 'You could stay with him. Always, I mean. Or for a long time.'

'Could you really advise that?'

'It's so much the issue that it deserves saying. Still – one shouldn't assume a greater sacrifice than one can gracefully sustain. As for advice –' She made a face, the kind of face Isabella had made when speaking of the doctor. 'People at a disadvantage are so tempted by envy or destruction. Ideally, one should get advice from someone who is at an advantage, not from –' She indicated the bed, the medicines, her condition.

At what greater advantage can you be, Sophie wondered, than to have come to the end of your life?

'Do you ever notice,' asked Luisa, 'how easy it is to forgive a person any number of faults for one endearing characteristic, for a certain style, or some commitment to life – while someone with many good qualities is insupportable for a single defect if it happens to be a boring one? I think . . . sometimes experience is like that, and that it matters to have committed yourself at one moment, even at great cost and disorder, and to know that you have that capacity. We can't be orderly all the time without becoming bores.'

They were both quiet for a long time, and Luisa closed her eyes. Watching her, Sophie noticed for the first time a resemblance to her mother, Luisa's half-sister. There had always been some physical similarity – the same pale skin drawn over high cheekbones, the same pale hair grown grey, and a strength and beauty of features that contradicted the pallid colouring. But a true resemblance, which would have depended on common judgements and responses, there had never been – for Sophie's mother, having at an early age observed the consequences of strong feelings, had prudently excluded herself from an encounter with them. She was cool and decisive about her own affairs; with her children she maintained a neutral position that from time to time she reinforced with sweeping pronouncements: 'I expect you're old enough to know your own mind,' 'I suppose you know what you're doing' – unlikely assumptions that would never have entered Luisa's head.

This very impersonality, which had distinguished Sophie's mother from Luisa in looks and had subtly divided the two sisters throughout their lives, was now for the first time to be seen on Luisa's face. Here the detachment was of a different quality, not merely because it was making its appearance for the first time (and it may be said that Luisa's eyes, closed as they now were, were infinitely more expressive than her sister's would have been wide open) but because it was directly connected to Luisa's disengagement from life and to her speculations on her own death. Sophie saw this and understood it, and turned her face away.

Luisa spoke, reaching out her hand again to touch Sophie. 'When do you mean to go?'

'Right away.' And then, retreating like Tancredi from what was unbearable, she said: 'In a few days.' She chose a day at random, knowing she would be bound by it. 'On Tuesday.' A tremor that could have been hers or Luisa's ran through their clasped hands.

'Listen,' Luisa said, drawing herself up in the bed and leaning on her elbow to look at Sophie, 'It may be better not to go.'

Sophie said: 'I must go.' She drew her hand away.

'But think of it –' Luisa began. Then she said: 'No – I'm sure you've thought of it too much. That's our indulgence, yours and mine, to think of things until we've thought the true meaning out of them and the need for any action.'

Sophie smiled. 'We're used to being serious.'

'Unlike Tancredi. . . . But think, my dear, of Tancredi.'

Sophie repeated: 'I must go,' and this time she gave her words an immediate significance by getting to her feet.

Luisa took her weight off her elbow and lay back on her pillow. At last she said: 'Will I see you again?'

'Before I go?' Sophie supplied. 'Of course. Perhaps tomorrow?' She looked about the room. 'Is there something you would like? Shall I close the window?' It seemed hard to leave Luisa without having been of any use to her, without having performed some small service for her or paid any deference to her illness. When she came back, tomorrow, she would show more concern for Luisa and talk about other things, about anything but Tancredi. She took Luisa's hand again. Having made up one's mind to suffer a great hurt, it was somehow disheartening, a disappointment, to be told it need not be borne and that some other way could be found, less lonely but harder, more imperfect but bearable. She stood over Luisa, trying to forgive her for causing such a disturbance. Then she laid the thin hand back on the sheet, as Tancredi had done. She waited a moment, awkwardly, and went out without speaking again.

I should have consoled her, given her courage, Luisa thought. Or I should have said nothing. Why should I try to persuade her to do otherwise? Because it would be one of those important deflections one can make of one's own choice? No, she is right, and I should have said nothing. But, heavens, when she stood there saying she must go, how like her mother she looked.

# Fourteen

Now I'm early, Sophie thought as she came down the stairs, and he won't be there. Because she had a sense of having, in Luisa's eyes, just repudiated him, she needed to see him at once. She didn't want to stay in the house – she passed no one in the corridor but there were voices in the downstairs rooms. The front door was open and she thought she would go out in the garden and wait for Tancredi.

When she came out of the house the car was there. It was still so early that she wondered at first if Tancredi had not left at all. Then she remembered that he had driven off while she was waiting to be let in. She went down the steps and over to the empty car as if it might offer her some information, but as she reached it she saw Tancredi farther off, in the garden.

He was standing at the end of a path, between a pair of poplars. His back was towards her. The overhanging leaves, lime and yellow, fringed and dappled his person so that he too looked like some tattered autumnal tree. He was smoking a cigarette and looking at a girl who was raking the pebbled garden paths, a girl from one of the nearby farms who came up occasionally to work at the house. She was short and strong, this girl, with black hair and a very young, very golden skin. She was wearing a dark-blue chequered dress, and from her throat a cheap gold cross fell forward on a chain. She knew she was being watched, and that gave a conscious and not at all displeasing grace to her actions. And Tancredi stood watching her with a cigarette held in his green-and-golden hand.

Far from being hurt at finding him like this, Sophie could not help thinking how immensely she had separated him from such simple flirtations and how long it must be before he was free again – free of affection or remorse, or the sense of guilt – to enjoy them. She called to him in a low voice from where she was standing. He turned round and smiled. He came up to her, throwing his cigarette down on the stones.

They walked back to the car. She said: 'I'm early. I didn't expect to find you here.'

He put her in the car, then went round to the other side. 'I drove into town,' he told her, getting in. 'But then it seemed best to come back and wait here. If I'd gone to the office I could only have spent a few minutes there.'

She imagined his littered desk, thought of the clients who, knowingly or unknowingly, stood to benefit by her departure. Now that a day was fixed for her going, she was absolved from these responsibilities. For a moment she felt almost an elation, an extraordinary happiness at being with him. When they reached the main road she leaned over to touch her shoulder to his, and laughed. 'It's just as it used to be,' she said.

He looked round and smiled at her. 'Used to be? Before what?'

'Oh, before –' she began. 'Before we were important

to one another. Before you began to look serious.'

They had climbed a low hill and now started down a curving road bordered by fields. 'Are we going home?' he asked her.

'Let's drive for a little while.'

At the foot of the hill he turned off on another road. 'You haven't told me about Luisa.'

Sophie said: 'They've sent for another doctor.' She felt some necessity to keep her morning with Luisa intact as long as possible.

He frowned. 'Is it bad then? Worse than we thought?'

Sophie nodded. Although he could not see this, he did not repeat his question. A moment later he asked: 'She spoke about you? I mean, about me? What does she say?'

'It was she who told me you looked serious.'

'She's always given me to understand that would be an improvement. What did you say?'

'I said –' There was a long pause, during which he did not prompt her. She resumed, then, in her shaken, alien's voice. '– that I would not be here much longer.' She put out her hand to steady herself as they turned a corner, then kept her palm pressed to the upholstery as if this might strengthen her voice as well. 'I said that I would be going on Tuesday.'

They were climbing another gentle rise, and to the left above them, winding through vineyards, a private avenue had come into view. This avenue was noticeable for its length – at least a mile of it could be seen from the road – and for being lined with oaks rather than with the usual cypresses or ilexes of the region. There were no gates to the driveway where it met the road, but at that point the trees were arched so thickly together that they made a close tunnel. As they drew level with this entrance Tancredi slowed down involuntarily and Sophie leaned across to look.

'What is it?' she asked him.

'A villa,' he said. 'An eighteenth-century villa.' They had passed the entrance, but he stopped the car.

She peered back into the drive, but the road wound upward beneath the mingled branches and disappeared on a curve of the hill without revealing the house.

'Shall we go in?' Scarcely waiting for her reply, he reversed the car and turned into the drive.

The rough surface was comforting after the urgent efficiency of the highway; among its dents and ridges they slowed to a walking pace. On either side grass grew high against the twisted trunks of the trees. When they had gone about fifty yards along the avenue, Tancredi parked the car at a place where the roadway widened slightly and where another car might pass. But nothing approached them in the driveway or from the road behind. Under the hospitable arch of green, sheltered from the light of these last curious days, they were silent in one another's arms.

Insects and birds resumed their interrupted life outside the car. A leaf or two fell on the windshield, and they heard the flourish of some small animal in the grass. All around them, across the countryside, men and women went about their work or sat down to their lunch, talked and laughed – or wept, as they wept now. Even in that luminous green she persevered, trying to fit this love into some immense, annihilating context of human experience, assailing it with her sense of proportion.

Tancredi, who knew more about proportion, lifted his

head from hers. 'What could be worse than this?' he asked. 'What could be worse?'

Not long ago he had thought it logical that she should leave him. In the face of this pain, it now seemed meaningless, an action deliberately performed against the only life they could be sure of, their present existence, in the name of a future that might never come, and that in any case must contain inapprehensible elements. It was not her former decision to leave that he found irrational but her ability, having reached this degree of suffering, to go through with it. Were human beings not endowed with the ability to reverse their own decisions – and were they not always at their most sympathetic and most judicious when they did so?

He withdrew from her. He leaned his arms on the steering wheel and lowered his head over them. What can be worse than this? he wondered. Unless when she is actually gone.

'It will be easier when I have actually gone,' she said. She put her arm across his shoulders and her cheek on his sleeve. 'This is the hardest – here, on this road this morning; this is the hardest. I promise you.'

He lifted his head. 'How can you do this?' he asked, in his ingenuous, inquiring way.

She said: 'I have thought of it all.'

He was aghast at such determination. He thought vaguely: She will ruin her life with this sort of thing – as if her life were some distant future thing she had yet to embark on. He sat for some minutes staring ahead into the roadway with her head on his shoulder.

At last he sat up, letting her arm slide down his back. He said: 'Do you think I have room to turn?'

She twisted round to look out her side of the car. 'It seems the only place, doesn't it?'

When she looked back at him he pulled out his handkerchief and carefully dried both sides of her face. 'My love,' he said. He put his handkerchief away and started the car.

'What is it like, the villa?' she asked, leaning forward once more to stare up the drive.

'Oh – it's a famous house.' Tancredi paused, with his hand on the brake. 'It fell into ruins in the last century. The family who owned it never came there and everything went to pieces. Then it was inherited by a distant relative who had always wanted it but never expected it would come to him – I forget how it came about. Anyone could tell you – it's a well-known story. And this man, though he had no family and never married, devoted his time, his fortune – his life, you might say – to putting it back in order, restoring the façade and the interior, having the grounds laid out again according to the original plan. ... It was his great passion. It was supposed to have ruined him. It was – what's the word?'

'A folly.'

'Yes. His folly.' He let the brake off and began to back the car slowly on to the grass.

'Is he dead now?'

'He died just after the war. He was very old. My father knew him – I met him once or twice.'

'What is it like,' she persisted, 'when you get up there?'

'Very beautiful, I'm told. There's a great hallway, entirely frescoed. A fine library, splendid rooms, furniture, carpets, tapestries, and so on. An orangery, and a small theatre where they used to have music and plays. And then, of course, outside – there are fountains, arbours, a wood, pleasure gardens.' He looked out his own window to make sure he had room. 'And a terrace with a view of what seems to be the whole world.' Now he had turned the car. They jolted down the rough path and in a matter of seconds they were back at the road. He halted again under the rim of the last trees, narrowing his eyes against the glare of the road and looking to left and right. 'I have never been there,' he said.

# Fifteen

The water froze that winter in the pipes and drains, in the canals, lakes, and rivers of Europe. Snow fell on palms and temples in Sicily; icicles hung in clumps from the petrified fountains of Rome; and Venice, apparently loose from her moorings, drifted in an arctic sea. It was a fearful winter, cruel to the poor and expensive for the rich. In its final weeks, when it had displaced every instinct except that of survival, the certainty that it must come to an end was recognized as something glorious, a marvel of Nature – the edge, in fact, that Nature has over human ills.

When the end did come, it brought a dangerous thaw and a flood of statistics – figures of deaths and losses, of temperatures and dates, of centimetres of ice and snow. It was the worst winter that had ever been – that is to say, the worst winter on record, which, of course, amounts to the same thing. Only the very old claimed to remember winters as severe, and that was no doubt due to the exaggerations of memory.

At the end of March, Sophie arrived on a plane from London and a train from Rome – too late for her purpose, because Luisa died that very day. Luisa had been three days in a coma and died – it was at once pointed out – without a struggle; without knowing; without, as it were, feeling a thing. When that is said of someone loved whose life has been consumed in the assimilation of knowledge and feeling, their death seems more pitiful, more grossly a levelling than ever. It was all over, as they said, in a second. And this consolation – which lacks authority, for how can we know whether death is instantaneous to the dying? – even suggests a betrayal, for there is something shocking about such submissiveness, such alacrity to be dispatched from lovers and dependents, from thought and sensation, trees and sky, from that all which is over in a single second.

In the brief instant which put an end, then, to Luisa's life, Sophie was fastening back the thick curtain of her railway compartment north of Rome. She had the carriage to herself; this alone would have made it an extraordinary journey, since it was a trip she had always made in hot weather with the curtains drawn, the luggage racks full, and every place taken. The passing countryside gave an impression of hopes falsely raised, for the advanced spring of Rome became more tentative with every northward mile. The budding trees and hedges disappeared within an hour and the land was bare – not wintry so much as swept bleakly clean. The very trees seemed to have been taken up, brushed off, and replaced. The roads and bridges, the banks of swollen streams showed up as sharply as incisions. There was, nevertheless, one flagrant assertion of growth – for in this gaunt scene of earth, stone, and wood the almond trees were blooming in torrents of pale flowers.

There were a great many stops. Even people must have been scarce in the vacant landscape, since few got on and none got off. The railway line travelled through hills all the way, but the hills, lacking their summer crops and foliage, were reduced in size and character, so that the land appeared more vast and low-lying, almost a plain. Farms were numerous, and from time to time a handsome villa put in an appearance. These houses, like the sheds and waiting rooms of the stations where the train stopped, showed the winter in the way that buildings do – they had the look of having just been through a war, were bedraggled, shrunken, and somehow turned inward in self-protection.

An uncle Sophie had not seen since she was a child, one of Luisa's brothers, met her in the evening at the station. Like all that family, he was tall, stooping, long-nosed, long-necked, and long-limbed. His only profound conflict – a respectable one, between his sentiments and his judgement – showed pleasantly on his defeated face. He arranged for Sophie's bag to be put in the car and, standing on the cold platform in the dark, he told her that Luisa was dead. He for his part thought this unknown young woman must have been ill herself, she looked so very pale and stared so very hard. However, she was coming from a northern country at the end of the worst winter on record and that possibly explained it; the winter had been bad enough here in the south – what must it have been like for her?

He coughed his polite cough and put his polite hand on her arm to lead her to the car. There was nothing now for them to discuss, any other topic seeming unsuitable and the obvious one having been exhausted. Sophie apologized, as they drove along the country roads, for bringing the old man out, and he answered quite sincerely: 'Oh, it was fortunate, really it was. It gave me something to do.'

She understood this at once when she entered the house, for inactivity greeted her at the front door. Relatives – a dozen or more of them – sat downstairs in corners of the drawing room and the library, sometimes talking leadenly of social events or politics or the opera, sometimes in restless silence passing the intractable minutes of that day. When someone dies a long-expected death, the waiting goes on for a while – the waiting for what has already taken place but cannot yet be properly comprehended or decently acted upon. And so these figures sat downstairs and resignedly leaned their heads back against bookshelves or propped their feet on worn upholstery, and waited for Luisa to die – that is, for Luisa's death to become a reality. Those who wept a little gained, in their spasms of grief, a small advantage over the others, for they were already embarked on the process of realization and eventual reconciliation.

Sophie was given a room high up at the back of the house. There were several bedrooms there that had not been used since Luisa's children were young and brought friends home to stay in school holidays. That the room had been kept for this purpose was still to be seen in the lightness and modesty of the furniture, the inexpensive bedspread of flowered cotton, and a touching selection of books on a single shelf – touching because no taste is so quickly dated as that of the young. There was no fireplace, and the room was warmed, after a fashion, by an electric radiator. The windows, paned and unshuttered, gave on to a dark valley, and at the end of this valley could be seen very clearly the lights of the town.

All the guests sat down to dinner at one long table. Like Sophie's room, the ultimate leaf of the table had not been used in years; having warped in storage, it left an awkward ridge beneath the tablecloth. A small chandelier was suspended over each end of the table, and in the centre was an unlit candelabra. The corners of the room remained in darkness, making a pale oval of the light. Paintings were dimly seen on the walls – a romantic landscape, an upturned urn spilling eighteenth-century flowers, an unknown warrior bursting out of his froggings.

Some of the women had changed their dresses in order to give themselves something to do, and each had with her a shawl, a small fur, or a velvet jacket; one old lady had even brought a rug for her knees. Seen together, these relatives, with their prominent, attenuated features and light colouring, resembled nothing so much as a group of collie dogs, lifting their muzzles to greet one another and twitching their fine-boned shoulders or shifting about in their delicate, nervous way.

Old Isabella waiting at table was too busy to cry. She softly and consolingly spoke to herself as she handed around the platter.

On these occasions no one can feel quite free of blame. It is, first of all, difficult to exonerate oneself from a sensation of having contrived to stay alive while some one else has perished, and from the awareness of having, no doubt, behaved imperfectly to the dead. And then, in order to balance the excess of feeling, the harshest aspects of one's nature are forced up to the surface of the mind, and there they jostle confusingly with genuine regret. There was not a person in the room who could prevent himself from thinking from time to time, in the crudest or most mercenary terms, of the possible effects of Luisa's death on his own life. Her two sons were taken aback to find how often their minds reverted to the disposition of the house and the land. Her brother, who had innumerable possessions of his own and had never in his life coveted anyone else's, found himself speculating on the fate of every object that met his eye. Her cousin reflected that she would no longer make these tiring journeys to the country several times a year. As they had all loved Luisa, they were at first distressed to find themselves harbouring such ideas, then explained them away as the natural result of stress, and were less surprised than bored when they constantly recurred. Thus each passed the evening in a process of self-censure, interpretation, and acquittal, and, rather than submit fully to their loss of Luisa, unwittingly dispossessed her with their eyes and in their minds.

Sophie was not exempt from this natural law and had her own way of deploring Luisa's death. After dinner she stood by the window of her room and leaned her forehead against the icy glass and tried, like the other guests in the house, to grieve for Luisa. It was too soon; the memories she deliberately summoned came in true shapes and colours, but were transfixed and lifeless – a splendid collection of lepidoptera. In their place, before long, she could see the dark shapes of hills facing the house and the lights of the town going up the end of the valley. She discovered that she could not think of Luisa without accusing her of desertion – How could you leave me now? Why have you done this? She had lost her crucial witness, for if Luisa had not shared Sophie's experience she had acknowledged it, and her continued existence had testified to it.

Sophie stepped back from the window, leaving the pane smudged with her breathing and the warm impression of her brow. Again she thought of Luisa's kindness, of her tender manner and her graceful mind. And her thoughts went on: Why have you done this? How could you leave me now?

The servants took turns throughout the night to sit up in pairs in Luisa's room. The women of the household and their relatives, having performed this service for the dead before, came prepared with knitting and mending and occupied themselves in this way while they talked in low voices. Occasionally they forgot where they were and for a few moments exchanged gossip with no sense of impropriety. However, the conversation had mostly to do with the past. There were some who remembered Luisa as a girl, others who had cared for her young children or nursed her husband in his final illness. In all these recollections Luisa was given an exaggerated advantage that would have made her smile. But this was a tribute paid not from hypocrisy but to her general impression on their memory; if she had not merited high praise on these particular occasions, she had so much deserved it in the rest of her life that it should be offered at every opportunity.

On the following morning crocuses were discovered in the grass. The gardener remarked on this when, like everyone else, he came upstairs to view Luisa's body. The winter was by no means over – everything would be late this year and some of the shrubs had died or must be cut back to the earth if they were to survive. But the day was splendid, the sun strong, and there was talk of bringing the orange trees out of doors if the weather continued.

Sophie heard these things said in the corridor as she left Luisa's room. She went downstairs and out of the house by the side door, not taking time to fetch her coat.

She had already decided to leave for home that day, taking an evening train to Rome, without waiting for the funeral, which was to be held the following morning. Passing through the garden she saw the crocuses flaring from the taut earth. When she came to the end of the path she sat down on a bench and, putting her elbow on her knee, shaded her eyes from the sun with her hand.

Unnecessary and distasteful as it is, the viewing of a dead body may be a last attempt at recognition. Just as the victims of crimes or accidents must be identified under the law by those in a position to verify their past existence, so that morning Luisa had been seen and acknowledged by her closest acquaintances: 'Yes, this is she – whom I knew.' If the ritual is intended to confirm in the living the realization of what has happened, it was less than successful – for the rooms and corridors of the house and the garden where Sophie now sat were to remain for a long time the scenes of Luisa's experience. No one, that morning, coming down the stairs or looking through a window or wandering into the kitchen for more coffee, could do other than see with Luisa's eyes – as if they themselves were performing these actions and looking on these things for the last time. Alerted to their own mortality, they observed all the more closely what Luisa had been cut off from.


'When you think of her condition,' said one of the collie dogs, 'this was the best thing.' The statement was made directly, without much expression, like a theme on which variations are shortly to be played.

One or two more guests had arrived in the night and were staying for the funeral. The lunch table was cramped and all around it elbows were touching, as if in some country dance.

Leaning forward, Sophie's neighbour took his turn. 'The best thing,' he agreed. 'All things considered.'

No one has the capacity to consider all things, even if he wished to. From all those things that force themselves on our attention, we select what we can bear to consider. And that was happening now.

There was a grateful murmur: 'The best thing.' It was like the response in a prayer.

The best thing, Sophie wondered. It is not in the least the best thing. The best thing, surely, would have been for Luisa to live to be ninety, in full possession of her faculties. How can this be the best thing?

It was, of course, the best thing because it was the only thing; it had happened. Anyone who would not now recognize it as the best thing must be looking for trouble.

An old man said bravely: 'She wasn't old.'

Giorgio, Luisa's son, said: 'It seems so wrong.' And – taking heart, as it were – 'It seems such a pity.'

'Ah – but given the circumstances, it was the best thing.' For the circumstances had been given – no one could dispute that.

'It was good of you to come.' This remark was addressed to Sophie.

'I'm only sorry,' she began, but all that was understood. So she said: 'I'm leaving this afternoon,' as if she were refuting her good intentions.

A taxi was coming for her at five. She would leave her bag at the station and spend an hour in the town before the train left. When she had explained this, there were offers to drive her, to keep her company, carry her bags, and put her on the train. 'Oh thank you,' she said, 'thank you,' lowering her eyes and following with her finger the gloss of the tablecloth. 'Thank you so much.' And at last, when it was all arranged, she said: 'No thank you. I'd rather go alone.'

It was an occasion when one could say such a thing.

# Sixteen

The women of the town were well dressed at all times, and in winter particularly distinguished in suits of English material and coats trimmed with beaver or astrakhan. Sophie, standing at a counter and warming her hands around her coffee cup, watched them go by in the street – stately women whose tawny or dark-gold hair curled from beneath their pretty hats or over their well-cut collars. The lamps had been turned on in the café, and these women passed across the lighted squares of window like figures across a screen, some carrying flowers or small parcels, some accompanied by a man or pulling a sagging child. If they seemed to Sophie that evening all more beautiful and younger than she, that was not what preoccupied her as she stood there.

She put a coin on the counter and went out herself into the street. She had left her handbag at the station with her luggage and she jingled loose money in the pockets of her coat. She went along slowly, like an unseasonable tourist, eyeing the buildings as if she had not seen them before but had heard a great deal about them. She kept her head attentively raised but seldom looked into the passing faces – nor did anyone take particular notice of her. When she came to the turn-off that led to the cathedral, she stopped and looked back down the sloping street, and again gave the impression of seeing all this for the first time, or of saying farewell to it after a long acquaintance – which is sometimes the same thing.

She strolled across the cathedral square. It was getting colder as the dark came down. The square had no motor traffic but was very busy with people on their way home – strange shrouded shapes from Goya, in heavy coats and mufflers that covered the mouth. Eyes met hers indifferently; she was of no interest to this hurrying cold-weather crowd. On the far side of the square she came to empty streets and locked doorways; soon the centre of the town would be like a deserted fairground. A clock began to strike and she stood still, separating her sleeve and glove, in order to alter her watch. Then she walked on in the direction of the station.

If she were to send a cable this evening before she took the train, there would be someone at the airport when she arrived in London – someone grateful for her cable, her arrival. This certainty affected her sadly, in much the same way as the sight of the pretty women walking in the street, and with an almost unbearable pressure of continuity. It was a piece of knowledge, arduously acquired, that one would rather not possess. Nevertheless, she began to compose the telegram in her mind and wondered if she had enough money with her to pay for it. And when she came to the last piazza, the unadorned square where the post office was, she crossed the street and went up the steps into the telegraph office.

The cable forms were stacked on a sloping counter under the pre-war yellow light of a hanging lamp. Sophie leaned on the counter, tore a page from one of the blocks of forms, and wrote her name in the space reserved for the sender's address. They were several people at the counter beside her. Every few minutes the street door swung open and the stuffy, stove-heated room was swept by night air. One or two crumpled forms lay about in admission of defeat, and the row of people concentrated on their scraps of paper as if this were an examination room. Sophie too stared at the trenchant little form and idly embellished with her pen the letters she had already written.

But her mind wandered, and in a little while she found she had written 'Dear' at the left of the page, as though she were beginning a letter. She tore this sheet off and threw it in the wastebasket, but did not begin another. After a moment she put the pen back on the desk and went out.

Tancredi's car was parked outside the post office. Sophie saw it at once – it was so much what she had been expecting that she glanced at the number to be sure it was his. Standing still on the post-office steps, she could see possessions of his scattered on the back seat, things she had never seen before because they belonged to the winter: a woollen scarf, a pair of brown leather gloves, a green felt hat – little clues to a daily life that she did not wish to imagine. Moved by the pain of seeing these things, she came slowly down the steps and stood beside the car. He must be very near, and she must go away before he came. For a second she closed her eyes trying to reconcile those two things. The knowledge of his proximity, the sight of his possessions compelled her to remember his face, his person, and the sound of his voice. Even the gloves on the seat of the car were shaped to his gesture.

She pushed back her cuff once more and looked at her watch – it was as if he had, at last, been late for their appointment. She put her cold hands back in her pockets and went on her way towards the station.

The rear coach of the train was filled by thirty or forty young soldiers being moved from one military encampment to another. They, and their ungainly equipment, were in the charge of an officer, a pink and portly man who left the train at each stop in order to stride importantly up and down the platform. (At one such stop, owing to the complicity of the guard, this *maresciallo* came near to missing the train, which started without warning.) The soldiers, like all soldiers on the move, were loud, ribald, and fairly cheerful – but they were also shabby, shy, and ignorant, their callow wrists and necks squirming in the ill-fitting clutch of their uniforms, their pale faces occasionally puzzled and humiliated like those of prisoners. From time to time one of the group would escape from the *maresciallo* and find his way into the other coaches. But, having made this intrepid journey, he would find himself too timid to speak to the passengers and, after loitering in the first-class corridor for a few minutes, would return to the fold smiling foolishly.

The soldiers were forbidden to leave the train, but at every station they pushed the windows down so that they could call to girls on the platform or buy chocolate bars from a barrowman or jeer in transparent asides at the striding *maresciallo*. When the train was still for a few minutes in this way, the bugler would begin to play – always the same air, an antiquated sentimental tune that belonged, perhaps, to a regional song. This wistful music filled the train and floated out on the cold dark station of every town they stopped at. The song never reached its conclusion, for the train would always start up again with the last refrain and the instrument would be violently shaken in the musician's mouth and grasp. But after each such depature, for a little while, the bugler tried to keep playing, to reach the end of the song; and these last notes, wobbling and swaying, persisted out of the station and into the countryside until the train, gathering speed, made it impossible to play any longer.